The First Lady of Tennessee

Allen Sircy

Published by Southern Ghost Stories, Gallatin, Tennessee

ISBN: 979-8-9988146-1-7

.

Table of Contents

The Letter

Present Day
January 20, 1861, Gallatin, Tennessee

The bedroom in the modest house on the Gallatin square was a haven of dancing shadows, warmed by the faint glow of a dying fireplace. The air held a quiet blend of woodsmoke and lavender, clinging to the room's personal touches—an old portrait on the wall, a Bible on a bedside table, and a large trunk in the corner, heavy with memories Eliza Allen had long kept locked away. At fifty-one, she was a fragile echo of her former self, her frame withered by illness, yet her eyes burned with a quiet dignity.

The door creaked open, and Susie, eighteen, slipped into the room, her petite frame alight with the unpolished grace of youth. Her chestnut hair caught the firelight as she moved cautiously to her mother's bedside, her eyes soft with love and worry. She sank onto the edge of the bed, wrapping Eliza in a gentle embrace, careful not to press too hard.

"Oh, honey, it's so good to see you," Eliza murmured, her voice warm but rasped by sickness. She pulled back, a mischievous twinkle sparking in her eyes. "Tell me, how many suitors do you have?"

Susie blushed, brushing a strand of hair behind her ear. "Oh, Mother," she said, laughter mingling with exasperation. "You know how busy my studies keep me."

The door creaked again, and Susie's father, a man in his fifties, gentle and worn, stepped inside. His weathered face softened as he looked at Eliza. "You comfortable, dear?" he asked softly, his voice laced with concern.

Nodding faintly, Eliza flashed a tired smile. "I'm fine, thank you."

He hesitated, then nodded. "I'll be downstairs," he said, and slipped out, the door closing with a soft thud.

A cough tore through Eliza, sharp and jarring. Susie's hand tightened on her mother's arm, her brow creasing. "Are you well?"

Eliza waved a trembling hand. "I'm feeling better. The cough's subsided a little since last week."

She leaned forward slightly, her curiosity reigniting as she studied her daughter. "Tell me, how are your studies at the Female Academy?"

Susie's face brightened, her shyness melting into enthusiasm. "My needlework's getting much better. Still not as fine as yours, though." She couldn't help but smile, her excitement bubbling over. "I struggled with the harp, but I've taken to the piano. Oh, I love it so. When you are feeling better, we could visit the Guilds. I'll play for you."

Eliza's face glowed with pride. "I'm so happy you're here," she said softly. Her eyes floated to the trunk in the corner, and she gestured with a frail hand. "There's something in there I'd like you to have."

Susie's curiosity flared. She rose and crossed to the trunk, her footsteps light on the creaking floorboards. Kneeling, she lifted the lid carefully, revealing a trove of old treasures—letters bound with ribbons, small boxes, and folded fabrics. Eliza's voice guided her from the bed.

"There's a dress in there that belonged to my mother. I wore it too, when I was your age."

Susie's hands moved eagerly, sifting until her

fingers brushed a folded white dress, its fabric soft and timeworn. "This one?" she asked, holding it up.

Eliza nodded, her smile wistful. "That's the one."

As Susie lifted the dress, an old letter slipped from its folds and fluttered to the floor. She bent to retrieve it, her brow furrowing as she unfolded the brittle paper and read aloud, her voice soft but clear. "'That I have and do love Eliza, none can doubt...'"

Eliza stiffened, her fingers clutching the quilt. The air thickened, the fire's crackle suddenly too loud. "You can put that back," she said tightly.

But Susie's eyes stayed fixed on the letter, her voice trembling as she continued. "'Eliza stands acquitted by me. I have received her as a virtuous wife, and as such I pray to God I may ever regard her...'" She stopped, her eyes snapping to her mother, disbelief carving lines across her face. "Mother?"

Susie reached for her mother's hand, her voice urgent. "Mother, what is this? You were married before Father?"

Eliza's eyes welled with tears, her breath catching as words eluded her. Susie glanced back at the letter, her voice a whisper as she read the signature. "It's signed Sam Houston."

She looked up, stunned. "Is this the governor of Texas?"

Eliza nodded faintly, her hands twisting in the quilt. She hesitated, then added, "Actually, at the time, he was governor of Tennessee."

Susie's mouth parted, her world shifting. "You never told me..."

"Dear..." Eliza's voice cracked, a plea and an apology woven into the word.

"What happened?" Susie asked, her voice soft but insistent, the letter still clutched in her hands.

Eliza's eyes shifted to the fire, the flames reflecting in her eyes as memories stirred, pulling her back to a night when she was young, when the world had felt both too large and too small, and a man named Sam Houston had walked into her life.

April 1828, Castalian Springs, Tennessee

The barn glowed with the warmth of lantern light, its rafters strung with flickering flames that cast a golden haze over a small crowd. The air buzzed with the murmur of conversation, the rustle of silk dresses, and the sharp twang of instruments tuning in the corner. Women in elegant gowns sat in clusters, their fans fluttering like butterfly wings, their eyes darting toward the large wooden doors with barely concealed anticipation. The scent of hay and polished leather mingled with the faint sweetness of cider, filling the space with a restless energy.

Eliza, eighteen and striking in her quiet way, sat near the edge of the gathering, her arms crossed tightly over her chest. Her dark hair was pinned neatly, framing a face that was beautiful but distant, her hazel eyes scanning the room with a skepticism that set her apart from the eager chatter. Beside her, Ann Boyers, nineteen and bubbling with excitement, leaned forward, her blonde curls bouncing as she fanned herself with exaggerated flair.

"Oh, isn't this exciting?" Ann said. "He should be here soon."

Eliza cast her a dry, unimpressed glance, one eyebrow arching slightly. "I suppose," she said, her voice flat, as if the prospect held no more allure than a chore.

Ann's enthusiasm didn't waver, but before she could press further, a hush fell over the crowd, sudden and sharp. The barn doors swung open, and Sam Houston strode in, his tall frame filling the space with an almost tangible presence. He was distinguished yet magnetic, his broad shoulders clad in a finely tailored coat, his dark hair swept back to reveal piercing eyes that seemed to command the room. Women straightened their postures, their fans stilled; men nodded with quiet respect, their murmurs fading. He moved with the ease of a man who knew his power, his smile both warm and calculated, as if he could charm the very rafters.

Eliza's breath caught, though she'd never admit it. He was a legendary figure, and he was only thirty-five years old.

The barn seemed to blur, the lantern light dissolving into a different glow, one born of sunlight and open skies, as her memory reached further back, to a time before she'd ever met him, to the boy who'd become the man who'd changed her life.

Colonneh

1811, Rhea County, Tennessee

The Cherokee village hummed with life, a vibrant tapestry of sound and motion. Children darted barefoot through the dust, their laughter ringing like bells. Elders sat in the shade, their hands weaving baskets with practiced ease, while smoke curled lazily from cooking fires, carrying the scent of roasted corn and herbs. The Hiwassee River shimmered nearby, its waters a constant whisper beneath the village's pulse.

Oolooteka, a wise and gentle chief in his fifties, walked slowly through the village, his presence as steady as the earth beneath his feet. Beside him strode Sam Houston, eighteen, lanky but determined, his frontier clothes patched and worn. His dark hair fell untidily over his brow, and his eyes, sharp and restless, drank in the world around him. He carried himself with a raw energy, as if he could outrun his own shadow.

Oolooteka gestured to the village, his voice fatherly yet instructive. "You see, Colonneh, the people here…" He paused, his hand sweeping toward the weavers, the children, the fires. "Each one knows their place, their duty."

Eliza's voice carried through the memory. "When he was a boy, his father died. He didn't like answering to his older brothers, so he left home and went to live with the Cherokee near Chattanooga."

Sam nodded, his chin lifted as if to project wisdom beyond his years. Oolooteka's eyes crinkled, a knowing chuckle rumbling in his chest. "But you..." he said, his words light but carrying weight, "you are not like them. You are a raven. A wanderer. Adaptable. Always watching for the next opportunity."

He grinned, tapping Sam's chest lightly with an affectionate hand.

Eliza's voice continued, a thread connecting past to present. The Chief liked Sam. Called him Colonneh, which was their word for Raven.

A sudden burst of movement interrupted them. Diana, a ten-year-old girl with dark braids and a mischievous smile, rushed toward them, clutching a bundle of wildflowers. "Uncle!" she called, beaming at Oolooteka before turning her wide, curious eyes to Sam. "Colonneh, you should smile more. Why must you always look unhappy?"

Sam rolled his eyes, but a grin tugged at his lips, betraying his attempt at stoicism. Oolooteka's hearty laugh echoed through the village, a deep, resonant sound that seemed to bind them all together.

◆ ◆ ◆ ◆ ◆ ◆

Sunlight reflected off the Hiwassee's rippling surface, the water cool and clear as Sam waded in, a spear clutched tightly in his hands. Nearby, a group of Cherokee men moved with practiced ease, their spears darting into the current to snag fish with fluid precision. Sam fixed his eyes on a silver fish darting beneath the surface.

He lunged, the spear slicing through the water. Splash! The fish slipped away, and Sam groaned. The men glanced over, their smirks and muffled laughs carrying across the river. From the bank, Diana's high-pitched giggle rang out, sharp and unrelenting. Barefoot, she ran to the water's edge, her braids swinging as she waded in, splishing and splashing toward Sam.

"Colonneh!" she called, her voice teasing. "Have you caught anything, or are you just playing in the water?"

Sam scowled, his cheeks flushing. "Get out of the water!" he snapped, his annoyance barely masking a grudging amusement. "You're scaring away the fish."

Diana grinned, undeterred, her splashing disrupting the river's calm. "Maybe the fish are scared of you…"

Sam shook his head, muttering under his breath as she laughed, her joy infectious. He waded back to the bank, his spear empty, his pride bruised but intact.

◆ ◆ ◆ ◆ ◆ ◆

Later that night, the teepee glowed softly, its fire casting a warm light across the woven walls. Oolooteka sat cross-legged, his eyes twinkling as he watched Diana, still brimming with energy, poke a stick into the ground, mimicking Sam's failed fishing attempts with exaggerated flair. Her giggles filled the space, a counterpoint to the fire's gentle crackle.

Sam entered, a basket of fish slung over his shoulder. He set it down with a dramatic flourish, his chest puffed with pride. Diana's eyes widened as she scurried over, inspecting the haul with a mix of awe and suspicion. "You caught all these?"

Sam grinned, his earlier frustration forgotten. "Perhaps next time I'll teach you — if you promise not to scare them all away."

Oolooteka's laugh rumbled, deep and warm, as Diana stuck out her tongue. Sam settled beside the chief, his expression softening as Oolooteka patted his back. "You are learning, Colonneh," the older man said, his voice rich with approval.

Sam's gaze shifted to Diana, who was happily sorting the fish, her chatter filling the teepee. A quiet warmth settled over him, a sense of belonging he hadn't felt since his father's death, as if this village, these people, had given him a home he'd never known he needed.

Present Day

The firelight danced in Eliza's eyes, its glow a tether to memories she'd long kept buried. Susie leaned closer, the letter from Sam Houston still clutched in her hands, its words a spark that had ignited a cascade of questions. "He lived with the Cherokee?" she'd asked, and now her curiosity burned brighter, her voice soft but eager.

Eliza's lips curved into a faint smile, though her eyes remained fixed on the flames. "Sam was never one to stay still," she said, her voice rasped by illness. "He left the Cherokee, chasing something bigger — a fight, a name, a place in the world. And when the call came, he answered." Her words trailed off, and the bedroom's quiet gave way to the clamor of a different time, a tavern thick with whisky and ambition, where a young man stepped into the shadow of war.

February 1812, Maryville, Tennessee

The crackle of the fire faded, replaced by the sharp tang of whisky and the raucous laughter of a Maryville saloon in 1812. Men crowded the tables, their faces weathered by labor and drink. Smoke curled from pipes, blurring the dim light that spilled from oil lamps hung on the walls. Into this chaos strode Sam Houston, now twenty, taller and broader than the lanky boy who'd fished the Hiwassee. His frontier clothes were patched but clean, his dark hair swept back, and his eyes, sharp and searching, scanned the room with a purpose that set him apart.

In a corner, an officer in a crisp militia uniform sat alone, his posture rigid, his gaze discerning. He looked up as Sam approached, sizing him up with a practiced eye — taking in the young man's height, the set of his shoulders, the quiet confidence in his step. Impressed, the officer rose, extending his hand.

Eliza's voice, gentle with age, recounted Sam's early life. "When hostilities commenced with the British in 1812, a call was put out for young men willing to fight. Oh, Sam was a fighter."

Sam clasped the officer's hand firmly. The tavern's noise seemed to fade, the moment charged with possibility.

Eliza's continued. "He rose swiftly through the ranks."

Horseshoe Bend

March 27, 1814, Tallapoosa County, Alabama

Dawn broke over a large hill in southeast Alabama, where General Andrew Jackson stood with 3,300 men — regulars, militiamen, and allied Cherokee and Lower Creek warriors — watching and waiting. Across a horseshoe bend in the Tallapoosa River, thin tendrils of smoke curled upward from a fortified Red Stick village nestled below. Jackson surveyed the scene, his eyes narrowing as he gestured sharply, issuing commands to the knot of officers gathered around him.

Among them stood Sam Houston, now in his twenties, clad in a worn militia uniform. His face was leaner, hardened by two years of service, but his eyes burned with the same restless energy. He listened intently, his hand resting on the hilt of his sword.

"Do you see the smoke?" Jackson said, his voice cutting through the morning chill. "Their forces are now concentrated in the rear. We attack now! Lieutenant Houston, you'll lead the first charge."

Houston nodded, his jaw tightening as he reached for his sword. Around him, other soldiers exchanged nervous glances, but Sam's eyes remained fixed on the village below, his resolve unshaken.

Eliza's voice carried the memory forward, tinged with solemnity. "Before General Jackson became a hero in New Orleans, he was leading the Tennessee militia into Alabama to stop an uprising of the Red Stick Creek Indians backed by the British Crown."

Chaos erupted as the battle began, a maelstrom of smoke and screams that swallowed the valley. Bullets ripped through the air, arrows thudded into the earth, and the acrid scent of gunpowder mingled with the metallic tang of blood. Sam Houston charged forward at the head of dozens of men, his voice rising above the cacophony. "Over here! Attack!" he shouted, his sword shining in the sunlight.

The soldiers scrambled over a barricade of fallen trees, their faces smeared with dirt and fear. Sam led the way, his movements swift, deflecting a tomahawk with a deft swing of his blade as he pressed onward, his men struggling to keep pace.

Eliza's voice, laden with the cost of memory, echoed through the chaos. "It was a bloody affair."

A Creek warrior emerged from the smoke, his musket raised. The shot rang out, and Sam stumbled, clutching his shoulder as blood seeped through his uniform. Pain flashed across his face, but he refused to fall, his jaw gritted with defiance. "Forward!" he growled, his voice gritted through the agony, urging his men on.

He struggled forward, his steps uneven but determined, until—thwack! An arrow pierced his groin, its barbed tip tearing through flesh. Blood poured from the wound, dark and relentless, and Sam collapsed, his sword slipping from his hand. Around him, the battle raged. Soldiers and warriors grappled in the mud, blades gleaming, blood splattering across the earth. Sam's face grew pale, his eyes defiant even as the world blurred, the chaos unfolding in a haze of pain.

Within hours, dust had settled over a field littered with broken bodies. The air was thick with gunpowder, smoke, and the putrid stench of death.

A weary doctor knelt beside Sam, his hands stained crimson as he pressed trembling fingers to the young lieutenant's neck. Blood soaked through Sam's uniform, pooling beneath him. His chest barely rose.

An officer hovered nearby, his face grim, his jaw clenched.

"He's lost too much blood," the doctor muttered, voice flat with exhaustion.

"Leave him," the officer said quietly, with finality. "There's nothing else that can be done."

The doctor nodded solemnly, wiped his hands on a soiled cloth, and moved on to the next fallen man.

Sam lay motionless, his skin pale as bone. Around him, the cries of the wounded faded, swallowed by the vast silence that came after slaughter.

As the sun slipped below the horizon, the battlefield grew still—eerily still. Then, from the quiet, came a faint rustling.

Sam's hand twitched.

His fingers curled into a fist.

Slowly, with effort that drew on something deep and defiant, his eyes fluttered open—clouded, bloodshot, but burning with a raw, unyielding will to live.

A passing soldier froze as his lantern's faint glow landed on Sam's battered form.

He wasn't dead.

Not yet.

Eliza's voice carried through the darkness. "Sam was a mighty, mighty man."

Sam sat up, gritting his teeth against the searing pain. He forced himself to his knees, his breath ragged. His gaze fell to the arrow still lodged in his groin. He grasped it, tugging weakly, and a scream tore from his throat as fire burned through his body. The soldier approached cautiously, his eyes wide with disbelief.

"Pull it out!" Sam rasped, his voice hoarse but commanding.

The soldier hesitated, taking a step back. "Lieutenant, you need a doctor…"

Sam drew his sword, its blade glistening in the moonlight, his hand trembling but resolute. "I said pull it out!" he barked.

The soldier gulped, kneeling beside him. His hands shook as he grabbed the arrow, tugging gently, but it held fast. "I'm sorry, sir," he said, his voice tight. "This is going to hurt."

With a sharp yank, he pulled the arrow free. Sam's scream shattered the night, his body convulsing as pain overwhelmed him. He slumped back, unconscious, his blood staining the ground.

Eliza's voice softened, a note of respect threading through her words. "His bravery was noticed by General Jackson."

By morning, the field hospital tent was filled with wounded men. Sam lay on a cot, his face pale but stoic, his shoulder tightly bandaged, his groin wound wrapped in fresh linen. A doctor worked methodically, tightening the dressings, while another tended to nearby patients, their moans a constant undertone.

Andrew Jackson strode in, his presence cutting

through the haze of suffering. He stopped beside Sam's cot, looking down at the young lieutenant with a mix of admiration and amusement.

"Lieutenant Houston, you are one stubborn man," Jackson said, his voice gruff but warm. "We thought death came for you, but you turned him away."

Sam looked him in the eye, his lips twitching faintly, too weak to smile. Jackson nodded, his lips curling into a faint, approving smile.

"Please do your best to care for this man," Jackson said to the doctor, his tone firm. "His prospects are very bright."

He gave Sam a final nod before turning and striding out.

"In the years after Horseshoe Bend, Sam's star rose under Jackson's mentorship, his wounds healed as his ambition grew."

On the Rise

May 1819, Nashville, Tennessee

The saloon buzzed with life, its tables crowded with men whose laughter and clinking glasses filled the air with a rough camaraderie. The scent of whisky and tobacco hung heavy, curling through the sunlight that streamed through grimy windows. In a back corner, Andrew Jackson and Sam Houston sat together, their heads bent close over a table littered with glasses and maps. Jackson, now a national figure, his face lined with the weight of battles won, spoke with quiet intensity, his gestures sharp and deliberate. Sam, in his late twenties, listened intently, his militia uniform replaced by a crisp suit, his eyes sharp with ambition and respect.

Eliza's voice wove through the memory, carrying the arc of their rise. "After his victory in Alabama, General Jackson was promoted. He turned the tide in New Orleans against the British and became a national hero. His influence carried Sam far."

Sam nodded at Jackson's words, his expression one of unwavering focus, as if absorbing every syllable of the older man's vision for a nation—and their place in it.

January 1828, Nashville, Tennessee

The governor's office in Nashville was a world apart from the battlefield, its polished wood and ornate furnishings a testament to power earned. Sam Houston, now in his mid-thirties, sat at a large desk, a pen poised above a document that bore the weight of Tennessee's future. His dark hair was neatly swept back, his broad shoulders clad in a tailored coat, but his eyes held the same restless energy that had driven him through war and ambition.

Eliza's voice, tinged with both pride and irony, carried the memory forward. "Jackson saw to it that Sam became district attorney and later governor of Tennessee."

Sam glanced out the window for a moment, the bustling city a blur beyond the glass, then returned to the paper before him. With deliberate care, he signed his name, the ink a seal on his ascent.

The Governor's Eye

Present Day

Susie sat on the bed beside Eliza, her wide eyes fixed on her mother, the letter from Sam Houston still clutched in her hands, its words now woven into a tapestry of battles and triumphs. Eliza leaned back against the pillows, a faint, bittersweet smile on her lips.

"When reelection loomed, his prospects looked dim. The General put pressure on him to find a wife — someone to make him seem more relatable to the common man."

Eliza stifled a soft chuckle.

"Every girl desired to be his wife. Well, every girl except me."

She closed her eyes, her expression a mix of pride and sadness, as if the weight of Sam's legend pressed against the quieter truths she'd carried all these years.

April 1829, Castalian Springs, Tennessee

The barn pulsed with energy, its rafters alive with the twang of a fiddle, guitar, and banjo weaving a tune that set feet tapping and skirts swaying. Lanterns hung from the beams, casting a warm golden glow over the crowd. The air was thick with the scent of cider and polished leather, laced with the eager chatter of elegantly dressed women whose fans fluttered like moth wings, their eyes darting toward the center of the room.

Elmore Douglas, in his twenties, tall and lean, stood out among the musicians, his fiddle tucked beneath his chin. His fingers moved with heartfelt precision, coaxing a melody that seemed to carry a quiet longing. His eyes scanned the crowd before moving on, as if searching for something—or someone.

Sam Houston strode confidently through the room, his large frame and tailored coat commanding attention. His easy smile and piercing eyes drew whispers and stares from the women, their voices a soft hum of admiration. He moved with the grace of a man who knew his power, his presence a spark that ignited the air.

Ann Boyers could hardly contain her excitement, her blonde curls bouncing as she leaned toward Eliza, her fan fluttering furiously. "He is more handsome than I imagined," she whispered, her voice bright with awe. "That sketch of him I saw in the paper doesn't do him justice."

Eliza sat beside her, her arms crossed, her expression distant. She'd rather be at home, lost in a book or the quiet of Allendale, yet she caught herself tapping her toes to the music, the rhythm sneaking past her defenses.

Sam moved through the crowd, greeting each girl with a politeness that felt effortless, his charm deliberate yet disarming. He paused before Ann, his smile warm. "And what is your name, my dear?" he asked.

Ann swooned, her curtsy a flourish of excitement. "I am Ann Boyers," she said. "It's a pleasure to meet you, Governor."

"Boyers?" Sam said, his brow lifting. "Does your father own the general store on the square?"

"Yes, he does," Ann replied, her cheeks flushing.

"I know Thomas," Sam said, his voice rich with familiarity. "He's a fine man."

He kissed her hand, the gesture gallant, but his eyes shifted, catching on Eliza seated nearby. Her posture was rigid, her expression unreadable, yet her quiet beauty struck him like a chord. He was smitten.

"My, you are lovely," he said, his voice softening. "I am Sam. What's your name?"

Eliza glanced at Ann, who nudged her eagerly. Reluctantly, she rose slightly, her curtsy stiff. "Eliza Allen."

She offered her hand, and Sam took it gently, pressing his lips to her knuckles. Eliza pulled back quickly, her eyes flickering with discomfort, but Sam, undeterred, let the moment linger, his smile unwavering.

"Allen?" he said, his interest piqued. "Are you kin to Robert Allen, the Congressman here in Sumner County?"

Eliza nodded, her voice clipped. "He is my uncle."

"Oh, your father is John of Allendale?" Sam pressed, his words warm with recognition.

"Yes," Eliza said, offering a polite smile that didn't reach her eyes.

Sam moved on, greeting the next girl with the same charm, kissing her hand before stepping to the center of the barn. "Shall we dance?" he called, his voice ringing with invitation.

The band struck up a lively tune, and couples paired off, their laughter and chatter filling the air as they began to dance. Sam took Ann's hand, leading her to the floor, but his eyes drifted repeatedly to Eliza, who sat stiffly at the edge of the room, her arms crossed, her foot no longer tapping. Ann noticed his wandering eyes, but she said nothing, her steps light as she followed his lead.

Elmore watched from the bandstand, his fiddle singing beneath his bow. His eyes found Eliza.

The song ended, and Sam bowed to Ann, his gallantry impeccable. Then, with a confident stride, he crossed to Eliza. "May I have this dance?" he asked, his voice warm but insistent.

Eliza hesitated, shifting uncomfortably in her seat. "I, I…" she began, her words stumbling.

"Please, Eliza," Sam said, his smile broadening. "You are much too lovely to be sitting here all by yourself."

Sighing softly, Eliza rose, her movements graceful despite herself. "Very well," she said, her voice tinged with resignation.

Sam grinned triumphantly, leading her to the dance floor. As they moved to the music, he showered her with compliments, his voice low and earnest. "Your beauty is unmatched in this room," he said. "From the very moment I saw you, I was captivated."

For a moment, Eliza softened, a quiet laugh escaping her lips, his charm breaching her defenses. But as the song ended and Sam bowed politely, her mask of cool detachment returned. She retreated to her seat, where Ann waited, her eyes wide with excitement.

"Did you see the way he was looking at you?" Ann said, her voice a conspiratorial whisper.

Eliza shook her head, dismissing her friend with a wave. "There are a dozen girls here," she said firmly. "What does the governor of Tennessee want with me?"

The band concluded the evening with a jaunty ditty. Elmore stepped forward, his fiddle tucked under his arm, his lean frame silhouetted against the lantern light. "Ladies and gentlemen, thank you for a wonderful evening," he said warmly. "Governor, it is always a pleasure."

His eyes remained on Eliza for a moment. She noticed, offering a small, fleeting smile, but the moment passed as Sam moved toward the band, shaking hands with the musicians, his presence still commanding the room.

The night air was cool, carrying the scent of hay and distant rain as guests filed out of the barn, their chatter and laughter spilling into the darkness. Eliza and Ann stood near the door, Ann's excitement undimmed, her fan still fluttering.

Sam approached, his smile as warm as the lanterns. "Good night, ladies," he said, his voice rich with charm.

Ann beamed, practically bouncing on her toes. Eliza offered a soft smile, edging toward the door, hoping to slip away unnoticed.

"Ann, please give your father my warmest regards," Sam said with a smile.

"I will," Ann replied brightly.

Sam's gaze shifted to Eliza, his expression softening. "Miss Eliza, may I speak to you?" he asked, gesturing toward the back of the barn.

Ann nudged her encouragingly. Eliza's heart sank, but she nodded and reluctantly followed Sam, the crowd's chatter fading behind them.

The barn's interior was quieter now, the music gone. Shadows pooled in the corners, broken only by the faint glow of a single lantern. Sam turned to face Eliza, his commanding presence softened by an earnestness that caught her off guard.

"I would like to call on you," he said, his voice steady but warm. "Would your father object if I did?"

Eliza hesitated, her mind racing. He was the governor, a man of status and charm, his name a legend across Tennessee. She chose her words with care.

"I do not think he would turn away the governor should he come to his door," she said, her eyes meeting his briefly before looking away.

Sam grinned, a flash of triumph in his expression. He tipped his hat, his movements gallant. "Splendid," he said. "I will see you soon. Goodnight!"

He strode off into the night, his figure swallowed by the darkness, leaving Eliza standing alone, her face a mixture of confusion and unease. The weight of his words settled over her, a promise she hadn't sought, a path she wasn't sure she wanted.

Across the barn, Elmore, still packing up his fiddle, watched the exchange. His tall, lean frame was silhouetted against the lantern light, his hands faltering as he tightened the strings, his eyes drawn to Eliza like a moth to a flame. The quiet intensity in his eyes betrayed a longing he didn't voice, his movements slowing as he lingered on her distant expression.

Standing nearby, Ann noticed Elmore's distraction.

She nudged him lightly with her elbow. "Elmore, you're going to snap that string if you're not careful," she said.

Snapping out of it, Elmore fumbled with his fiddle. "Oh, sorry," he said softly.

Ann's eyes sparkled with mischief. "You were watching her, weren't you?"

Guarded, Elmore offered a nervous smile, his hands busy with his instrument. "I…" he began, but his words trailed off, his glance darting back to Eliza.

Eliza, as if sensing his gaze, turned slightly, their eyes meeting briefly across the barn. Elmore cleared his throat, hastily packing his fiddle, and rushed toward the door.

Eliza and Ann walked side by side a short distance behind him. Ann's curiosity was evident, her glance darting to Eliza, waiting for her to speak.

"Well?" Ann prompted, her voice eager.

Eliza sighed, her reluctance clear. "He said he'd like to call on me," she replied flatly.

Ann's eyes widened in delight. "Eliza! That's wonderful!" she exclaimed. "What did you say?"

"What could I say?" Eliza replied, her voice tinged with resignation. "He's the governor of Tennessee."

Ann grinned knowingly, her excitement undimmed. "While you were busy with the governor, someone else couldn't stop looking at you."

Eliza frowned slightly, confused. "Who?"

Ann began playing an invisible fiddle, her movements exaggerated, her smile wide. "The fiddle player," she said. "His name is Elmore Douglas. He works in my father's store. He's quiet, but kind."

Eliza's expression softened, a faint curiosity stirring. "I did not notice," she said quietly, her voice almost a whisper.

"Maybe you should."

Eliza offered a polite smile but said nothing more.

Present Day

The bedroom was quiet, the fire's soft glow casting a warm light across Eliza Allen's frail form. She reclined against a nest of pillows, her face illuminated by the flames, her eyes carrying the weight of years unspoken. Susie sat beside her, the letter from Sam Houston resting in her lap, its words a bridge to a past that still stirred her mother's heart. Her brow puckered, her voice soft but insistent. "Why didn't you tell him no?" she asked, her question cutting through the quiet like a blade.

Eliza's lips curved into a faint smile, tinged with the irony of hindsight. "I was young, and he was charming," she said, her voice rasped but clear. "You know, he asked if father would object. He did not ask if I would…"

A chuckle escaped her, light but fleeting, turning into a cough that shook her fragile frame. Susie's eyes widened, a mix of concern and awe as she watched her mother. Eliza stared at the fire, the flames conjuring a bustling town square, a day when laughter and peaches hid the weight of choices yet to come.

Peaches and Possibilities

June 14, 1828, Gallatin, Tennessee

The Gallatin town square hummed with life, its dirt street alive with the creak of wagons and the chatter of merchants. Horses snorted, their hooves kicking up dust that mingled with the warm scent of freshly baked bread wafting from a nearby bakery. Vendors called out, hawking their goods, while women in bonnets and men in broad hats wove through the crowd.

Eliza walked side by side with Ann, their laughter ringing out as they navigated the bustling square. Eliza's dark hair was tucked beneath a bonnet, her hazel eyes bright with the ease of the moment. Ann, her blonde curls bouncing, radiated enthusiasm, her fan dangling from her wrist as she pointed eagerly to a storefront ahead. A hand-painted sign read "Boyers General Store," its letters bold against the weathered wood.

"Come, father was expecting a shipment of peaches today," Ann said, her voice bright with anticipation. "I'd love to have one."

Eliza shrugged, her indifference softened by a willingness to indulge her friend. "Very well," she said lightly as they crossed the street.

The store was a treasure trove of goods, its shelves lined with jars of preserves, bolts of calico, and barrels brimming with flour and cornmeal. Thomas Boyers, a warm and welcoming man in his fifties, stood behind the counter, his face breaking into a grin as he spotted the girls entering.

"Well, if it isn't my little peach come to check on

her peaches!" he said, his voice rich with affection.

Giggling, Ann rushed to give her father a quick hug. Thomas turned his friendly gaze to Eliza. "Eliza, it is good to see you!" he said. "Would you like one too?"

Eliza smiled politely, her reserve softening under his warmth. "Yes sir, if it's not too much trouble," she said.

Thomas strode to a crate brimming with ripe peaches, their golden skins glowing in the sunlight that streamed through the window. He selected two with care and handed them to the girls. "Here you go," he said, his grin widening.

The girls bit into the peaches, their juices running down their chins in sweet rivulets. They tried to eat delicately, but the fruit's abundance defied them, and they dissolved into giggles, wiping their faces with their sleeves like children.

Thomas chuckled, leaning against the counter. "You two look like you're having a peach-eating contest," he teased.

Eliza laughed, her eyes sparkling. "If we are, I think Ann's winning," she said, glancing at her friend, whose face was smeared with juice.

Everyone laughed as Ann wiped her face again, her giggles infectious. Eliza's laughter faded into a practical thought, her mother's voice echoing from the previous night's dinner. "Mr. Boyers, do you have any cornmeal?" she asked. "Mother mentioned we were running low last night."

"Why certainly," Thomas said. "How much do you need?"

"A couple of pounds should be enough," Eliza replied.

Thomas strode toward the backroom, his voice carrying as he called out. "Elmore, will you please put five pounds of cornmeal in a bag for Miss Allen?" he shouted.

"Yes sir," came a muffled reply from the back.

Ann, still savoring her peach, glanced at her father with a hopeful smile. "Father, may I have another?" she asked.

Thomas smiled, his affection evident. "Of course, dear," he said. "Eliza, help yourself if you'd like one."

Ann plucked another peach from the crate, her enthusiasm undimmed. Eliza shook her head, her smile gentle. "They're delicious, but I think one is enough for me today," she said.

Elmore emerged from the back room, a neatly tied sack of cornmeal in his hands. His tall, lean frame moved with a quiet grace, his dark hair slightly tousled from work. He approached Thomas, Ann, and Eliza, who stood with her back turned, examining a bolt of blue fabric on a nearby shelf.

"Here you are, sir," Elmore said, his voice steady but soft.

Eliza turned at the sound, and their eyes met. For a brief moment, the world seemed to slow, the store's bustle fading into a hush. Elmore's face flushed slightly, but he couldn't help smiling. Eliza, caught off guard, returned the smile shyly, her fingers tightening on the fabric.

Oblivious to the moment, Thomas nodded. "It's for Eliza," he said.

Elmore quickly handed her the sack, his fingers brushing hers lightly, a fleeting touch that sent a spark through the air. "How much do I owe you, Mr. Boyers?"

Eliza asked, her voice steady despite the sudden warmth in her cheeks.

"Oh, I will see your mother later this week," Thomas said, waving a hand.

"Thank you," Eliza said, adjusting the sack in her arms.

Thomas casually glanced at Elmore.

"Elmore, do you want to carry that sack to their wagon?" he asked.

Elmore straightened, an eager light in his eyes as he took a half step forward. "I'd be happy to…" he began, his voice earnest.

Eliza's eyes widened, a nervous flush creeping up her neck. "Oh, no, thank you," she said quickly. "We'll manage."

Elmore's enthusiasm dimmed slightly, his shoulders sagging as he nodded, a faint disappointment flickering across his face. Eliza adjusted the sack, her movements brisk, as if to dispel the moment's intensity. Ann, watching closely, noticed the chemistry between them, her lips curving into a knowing smile.

Eliza and Ann walked side by side through the square, their steps light despite the weight of the sack of cornmeal in Eliza's arms. The bag strained her grip, its bulk shifting with each step, but she held it firmly, her chin lifted with quiet determination.

Ann glanced at her, a grin spreading across her face. "You know, Elmore would have been happy to help you," she said, her tone teasing, her eyes sparkling with mischief.

Eliza adjusted the sack, her arms aching as she shifted it to her other side. "It is no trouble at all," she said, her voice strained but resolute, though the effort was obvious.

Stifling a laugh, Ann's amusement bubbled over. "He's sweet, isn't he?"

Eliza glanced back toward Boyers General Store. Through the glass, she caught sight of Elmore behind the counter, following them down the street. Their eyes met again, a brief, electric moment that sent a flush to her cheeks. She quickly looked away, her heart quickening as she focused on a horse and buggy coming toward them. "He seems nice," she said softly.

Taking a bite of her second peach, Ann laughed as juice dripped down her chin. Eliza noticed and began to giggle as Ann wiped her face with a sleeve.

◆ ◆ ◆ ◆ ◆ ◆

The grand hallway of Allendale welcomed Eliza with its polished wood paneling and the stern gazes of ancestral portraits lining the walls. The air was cool, scented with beeswax and old wood. Clutching the sack of cornmeal, Eliza pushed the door open with her shoulder, her steps echoing in the hallway.

From the parlor, a burst of laughter broke the stillness, followed by the rapid patter of footsteps. John Allen, in his fifties, wiry and brimming with nervous energy, rushed out to greet her, his eyes alight with an excitement that set her on edge. "Eliza, dear, we have a visitor," he said, his voice practically vibrating with anticipation.

Eliza tilted her head, sensing something unusual in his manner. "Who is it, father?" she asked, her brow furrowing as she adjusted the sack in her arms.

John didn't answer immediately, instead gesturing

urgently for her to follow. He disappeared into the parlor, leaving Eliza in the hallway with a puzzled look on her face. She hesitated, then followed, her curiosity tinged with unease.

When Eliza entered the parlor, she found her mother, Laetitia Allen, sitting on a couch, her laughter filling the room like a melody. Opposite her stood Sam Houston, his hand pressed to his chest as if measuring an invisible figure.

"And when Mr. Van Buren talks about standing up for the little guy, you can tell he speaks from personal experience!" Sam said, trying not to laugh.

Laetitia roared with laughter, dabbing her eyes with a handkerchief. Sam joined in with a deep belly laugh, but as the governor turned, he caught Eliza standing in the doorway, the sack of cornmeal clutched tightly in her arms. His laughter broke off sharply, replaced by a brilliant smile that seemed to light the room.

Laetitia's face brightened further. "Eliza, the Governor came to visit us!" she said, her voice warm with pride.

Eliza looked to her father, who stood nearby, practically bouncing on his heels, his excitement barely contained. "He will be joining us for dinner," John added, his words tumbling out in a rush.

Shifting uncomfortably, Eliza's eyes darted between her parents' eager faces and Sam's steady smile. The sack of cornmeal felt heavier. Sam stepped forward, his charm unshaken, his presence filling the room.

"Miss Eliza," he said, his voice smooth as he extended a hand, his smile widening with an assurance that left no room for retreat.

Present Day

Sitting on the bed, Susie leaned forward eagerly, the letter from Sam Houston crinkling in her hands. "The governor of Tennessee came to your house to court you?" she asked, her voice a mix of awe and disbelief.

Eliza smiled faintly, her voice calm but laced with a touch of irony. "Yes, it was quite overwhelming," she said, looking to the fireplace.

Susie's eyes sparkled, her imagination alight. "Grandfather must have been jumping over the moon," she said, a grin spreading across her face.

Shaking her head, Eliza chuckled softly, the sound fading into a wistful silence. "Oh, my parents were beside themselves," she said, her voice softening. "The governor needed a wife, and Father thought I needed a husband."

Her laugh faded, her eyes drifted to the flames.

June 14, 1828, Gallatin, Tennessee

The dining room at Allendale was a vision of understated grandeur, its long, polished table shined under the soft light of a chandelier. Fine china and silver sparkled atop a crisp white tablecloth, set for four, the air scented with the savory aroma of baked ham. Eliza sat stiffly, her hands folded in her lap, her dark hair neatly pinned, her hazel eyes fixed on the window rather than the man across from her. John Allen sat to her left, his excitement barely contained, while Sam Houston, occupied the seat directly opposite.

Laetitia entered with a silver tray, the baked ham steaming as she moved around the table, carefully placing slices on each plate. Her stately demeanor was softened by a beaming smile, her excitement radiating as she served Sam, a guest of rare distinction.

Sam regaled the table with anecdotes and stories from his travels. His voice was warm and engaging, his charm as effortless as the sunlight streaming through the windows. John and Laetitia laughed heartily, but Eliza forced a polite smile, her discomfort visible in the tight set of her shoulders. She avoided looking at the governor, but his attention was relentless, glancing at her every so often, a silent invitation she couldn't ignore.

As Sam shared a story about falling off his horse, a quiet snicker escaped Eliza, her defenses cracking under the warmth of his humor. She caught herself, lips pressing together to stifle a fuller laugh—but Sam noticed. His smile broadened, his gaze holding just long enough to make her glance down, her composure fluttering like a leaf in the wind.

That moment hung between them, unspoken but

not unnoticed, carrying through the rest of the evening like a delicate thread. Later, as the night drew to a close, the grand hallway of Allendale glowed with the soft light of oil lamps. The family gathered at the door to bid Sam farewell.

John and Laetitia stood beaming, their satisfaction unmistakable — as if something long hoped for had quietly taken root.

"Governor, it has been an honor," John said, his voice brimming with enthusiasm, his wiry frame practically vibrating.

"The honor is mine," Sam replied graciously.

John and Laetitia exchanged a knowing glance, then excused themselves, their footsteps fading as they retreated into the house, leaving Eliza and Sam alone in the doorway. Sam turned to her, his commanding presence softening, his eyes warm with a sincerity that caught her off guard.

"There is a dinner next weekend being held for me in Nashville," he said gently. "Would you do me the honor of accompanying me?"

With her mind racing Eliza hesitated. She didn't want to go, her heart recoiling from the spotlight of his world, but the weight of societal expectations pressed against her — her parents' delight, the governor's status. Her silence stretched, her fingers twisting the fabric of her skirt.

Sam smiled gently, sensing her reluctance. "Your uncle will be present," he added reassuringly.

The mention of Uncle Robert tilted the scales. Eliza swallowed, her voice steady but soft. "Yes, Governor, I would be happy to join you," she said, the words feeling heavier than she intended.

Sam chuckled, pleased, his eyes crinkling with warmth. "Please, call me Sam," he said.

He leaned in, kissing her cheek. Eliza stiffened, her breath catching, but she didn't pull away. "Good night, Miss Eliza," Sam said, before stepping out into the night.

Eliza stood in the doorway, her hand brushing her cheek, her thoughts a whirl of wonder and hesitation. For a moment, she pondered a life in the upper crust—balls in Nashville, a governor's residence, a name that carried weight across Tennessee. But the vision felt distant, like a dress that didn't fit.

The momentary silence was broken by Laetitia's delighted voice, bursting into the hallway like a spring breeze. She practically danced toward Eliza, her eyes shining with excitement. "Well, Eliza, that went perfectly!" she exclaimed, gleaming with joy. "Did you see the way he looked at you? I do believe you've caught the Governor's eye."

Walking slowly into the parlor, Eliza's mind still raced. Laetitia followed, oblivious to her daughter's internal conflict, her steps light with triumph. "You must tell me everything!" she said impatiently. "Did he really ask you to accompany him to Nashville? He's such a fine gentleman. And so handsome too!"

Eliza glanced out the window, the night beyond a canvas of stars, her expression a mix of wonder and hesitation. "He is a gentleman…" she said quietly, her voice trailing off. "And yes, he is quite handsome, but I don't know, Mother. His position, his power… I don't know if I want that life."

Laetitia laughed softly, a knowing smile spreading across her face as she moved closer, resting a hand on Eliza's shoulder. "Oh, my dear, you don't need to want it—just accept it," she said, her tone sweet but with a touch of authority. "It's a life of comfort, respect, and status. Think of the possibilities, Eliza! You would be the talk of Nashville, and your future—secure, full of prestige. He is a man who can offer you everything."

Eliza's brow furrowed, her skepticism rising. "But what if that's not what I want?" she asked, her voice soft but firm. "What if I don't want to live in that world? My home is in Gallatin."

Trying her best to smile, Laetitia pressed on, her voice earnest. "I only want the best for you, my darling," she said.

Eliza lowered her eyes, her fingers now fiddling with the hem of her sleeve, her thoughts a tangle of doubt and fear. "It's not just that, Mother," she murmured. "It's… I don't know him. Not really. How can I know if I'm meant for a life with him?"

Laetitia sighed softly, taking Eliza's hand and guiding her to sit on the sofa, her touch both comforting and insistent. "You will, my darling," she said sincerely. "You will get to know him. You'll see the goodness in his heart, in his ambition, in his desires. Men like him—men of power—are not often easy to understand. But they are the ones who shape the world. And you will have a hand in shaping it with him. I know it's hard, but think of your future, your family…"

Eliza swallowed hard, the weight of her mother's words pressing against her chest. A pang of frustration stirred within her, as if a part of her was being tethered to a future she didn't choose. "I don't want to be just a part of a grand plan, Mother," she said softly. "I want… more."

Laetitia squeezed her hand, a touch of impatience

creeping into her voice. "You will, Eliza," she said assuringly. "Just trust me. This is what you've been raised for. You've seen the life your father and I have made. You can have that, too—only better. Don't turn away from this, darling."

Eliza leaned back on the sofa, her eyes shifting to the window again. The weight of the conversation hung in the air, unresolved.

"I'll go to Nashville, Mother," she said after a long pause, her voice quiet but firm. "For the dinner."

Laetitia's face brightened, her delight spilling over as she hugged Eliza tightly, completely oblivious to her daughter's inner turmoil. "Oh, how wonderful, Eliza!" she exclaimed, her voice gleeful.

As Laetitia walked away, humming with happiness, Eliza remained seated, her eyes fixed on the window, pondering her future.

Royal Blue Bolts

June 22, 1828, Gallatin, Tennessee

The Gallatin square shimmered under a bright afternoon sun, its dirt street alive with the clatter of wagons and the calls of merchants. The air was warm, scented with dust and the faint sweetness of blooming jasmine, as women in bonnets and men in broad hats wove through the crowd, their voices a lively hum of trade and gossip. Ann Boyers walked beside Eliza Allen, her blonde curls bouncing as she chattered animatedly, her fan dangling from her wrist. Eliza listened with half an ear, her dark hair tucked beneath a simple bonnet, her hazel eyes distant, her mind racing.

"Oh, you're going to be the talk of Nashville in your new dress!" Ann said, her voice bright with excitement. "Everyone will envy you."

Eliza sighed, her steps slowing as she adjusted her shawl. "It's just a dinner," she said flatly, though a faint weariness underscored her words.

Ann raised an eyebrow, a smirk playing on her lips. "A dinner?" she said. "With the governor of Tennessee? Eliza Allen, that's not just a dinner."

Eliza rolled her eyes, but a small smile crept onto her lips. They approached Boyers General Store, its hand-painted sign bold against the weathered wood, the promise of fabric and distraction drawing them closer.

The bell above the door jingled as Ann and Eliza stepped inside the store. Thomas Boyers stood at the counter, chatting with a customer, his face breaking into a warm smile when he saw the girls.

"Ann! Eliza!" he called, his voice rich with affection. "What brings you back so soon?"

Ann's eyes sparkled as she stepped forward, her enthusiasm undimmed. "We need some fabric," she said. "Eliza has to have something special for the governor's dinner."

Thomas raised an impressed eyebrow, his glance shifting to Eliza, who stood slightly behind Ann, her expression reserved. "Well, you've come to the right place," he said. "We've just received some fine new bolts from Nashville."

Before he could move to assist them, Elmore emerged from the back room dressed nicely in a pressed white shirt and neat trousers. His dark hair was combed back, his appearance polished. Her eyes caught his first, a brief moment of recognition passing between them before she looked away, her fingers tightening on her shawl.

Ann noticed, her grin widening. "Well, don't you look fancy, Elmore," she teased. "What's the occasion?"

Elmore smiled shyly, his eyes affixed to Eliza as he answered, his voice soft but steady. "I'm playing the fiddle at church this evening," he said.

Ann's smirk deepened, her fan snapping open with a playful flourish. "That explains it," she said. "I didn't think you'd dress up for us."

Elmore chuckled softly, a warmth in his eyes, but he couldn't take his eyes off Eliza, who stood quietly. "You play beautifully," she said softly, her voice almost a whisper. "At the barn dance… I really enjoyed it."

Elmore's eyes widened slightly, surprised but pleased by her compliment. "Thank you," he said, his voice earnest. "I'm glad you liked it. The fiddle's in the back if… well, if you'd like to hear something."

Ann's enthusiasm surged, her eyes darting between them. "Oh, we'd love to!" she said, her voice bright. "Wouldn't we, Eliza?"

Eliza glanced at Ann, flustered but intrigued, a spark of curiosity breaking through her reserve. "If you don't mind," she said quietly, her tone hesitant but genuine.

Elmore grinned, a quiet joy lighting his features as he gestured toward the back room. "Right this way," he said, leading them past the shelves into the back of the store.

The back room was a cozy, cluttered haven, its shelves stacked with sacks of grain and cornmeal, barrels of molasses, and crates of goods waiting to be unpacked. A single window let in a shaft of sunlight, illuminating Elmore as he carefully set his fiddle case on a table. Ann and Eliza stood nearby, Ann's enthusiasm a bright spark, while Eliza's reserved curiosity softened her usual guarded demeanor.

Opening the case, Elmore lifting the fiddle with a reverence that spoke of years spent coaxing melodies from its strings. He positioned it under his chin, his dark hair falling slightly over his brow, his lean frame relaxed yet focused. "This is a song called 'Araby's Daughter,'" he said, his voice soft but clear, a hint of pride in his tone.

He moved his fingers and bow gracefully, the first notes of the tune filling the room with a haunting, lilting melody. The music wove through the cluttered room, its warmth wrapping around them like a shared secret. Ann tapped her foot to the rhythm, her grin wide as she glanced at Eliza, but Eliza was transfixed, her hazel eyes fixed on Elmore as the notes washed over her. The melody seemed to pull at something deep within her, a longing she couldn't name, her breath catching as the music swelled.

When the tune ended, Elmore lowered the fiddle, his cheeks flushed but his expression proud, as if the song had been a gift offered to the room. Ann clapped, her hands a burst of sound in the quiet. "That was wonderful!" she exclaimed, her voice bright.

Eliza nodded, her voice soft but genuine, her usual reserve giving way to a rare sincerity. "It was beautiful," she said. "You play with such… feeling."

Elmore glanced at her, his smile shy but pleased, a warmth lighting his eyes. "Thank you," he said earnestly. "It means a lot to hear that."

Eliza tilted her head slightly, a hesitant curiosity in her voice. "I've always admired musicians," she said. "I've often thought I'd like to play, but… I'm not musically inclined."

Without missing a beat, Elmore stepped forward, holding the fiddle out to her, his movements confident yet gentle. "Here," he said. "Try it."

Eliza blinked, startled, her hands rising instinctively. "Oh, I couldn't possibly—" she began, her voice faltering.

"Of course, you can," Elmore said, his tone encouraging.

He placed the fiddle in her hands, his touch careful yet steady, the wood warm against her fingers. Eliza held it awkwardly, her posture stiff, unsure of where to start. "I don't even know where to begin," she said, a nervous laugh escaping her.

Stepping closer, Elmore moved behind her, his presence calming. He leaned down slightly, his arms brushing hers as he gently guided the fiddle under her chin. "Hold it like this," he said, his voice soft, almost a whisper.

He raised her left arm, his hand holding hers as he positioned her fingers on the strings, his touch light but purposeful. "These fingers go here," he said. "Now, take the bow…"

He lifted the bow, placing it in her right hand, and adjusted her grip, his fingers brushing hers for a brief moment. "Gently, now," he said. "Draw it across the strings, like this."

Guided by his hands, his fingers steady on the strings, Eliza moved the bow. A hesitant, wavering note emerged, followed by several more uneven but recognizable tones, each one a small triumph. Ann clapped her hands together, laughing with delight. "Eliza! You're playing!" she exclaimed.

Eliza let out a surprised laugh, her face lighting up with a mixture of pride and embarrassment, her usual reserve melting in the warmth of the moment. "It's not very good," she said, her smile wide despite her words.

Smiling, Elmore's eyes crinkled with encouragement. "For a first try? It's great!" he exclaimed.

They laughed together, the sound filling the small room, a shared joy that seemed to shrink the world to just the two of them. Eliza looked up at Elmore, her smile softening as their eyes met, an unspoken connection sparking in the quiet. For a moment, the weight of Nashville, Sam, and her parents' expectations felt distant, replaced by the simple warmth of a shared melody.

The door creaked open, breaking the spell. Thomas Boyers entered, holding a ledger, his face creasing with an amused expression as he took in the scene. "Well done, Elmore," he said approvingly. "I see you've found yourself a student."

Eliza quickly stepped back, lowering the fiddle, her cheeks flushing as she handed it to Elmore. "He's a very patient teacher," she said, her voice steady but tinged with warmth.

Thomas chuckled, shaking his head. "Elmore, as much as I hate to interrupt, I've got customers up front."

Elmore straightened, his smile fading slightly as he nodded. "Yes, sir," he said, gently taking the fiddle from Eliza, his fingers brushing hers as he placed it back in the case. He turned to her, hesitating for a moment, his expression soft. "It was nice seeing you again, Eliza."

"And you," Eliza replied, her tone genuine, a small smile curving her lips.

Elmore offered a polite smile before exiting, his footsteps retreating to the front of the store. Ann watched him go, then turned to Eliza with a sly grin. "He really likes you," she said, her voice a conspiratorial whisper.

Eliza shook her head quickly, brushing past Ann's comment as she moved toward the front of the store. "Come on," she said, her tone brisk. "I need to get that fabric for mother."

Making their way to the front of the store, Eliza scanned the bolts of fabric behind the counter. She pondered for a moment and then pointed to a bolt of royal blue, its rich hue catching her eye. "That one," she said, her voice light.

Thomas, standing behind the counter, eagerly pulled the bolt down, cutting and folding the fabric with practiced ease. "How much is it, Mr. Boyers?" Eliza asked, reaching for her purse.

Thomas waved a dismissive hand, his smile warm. "On the house, Eliza," he said. "For the governor's dinner."

Eliza's smile wavered slightly, the mention of the dinner pulling her back to the weight of expectations, but she nodded. "Thank you!" she said politely as she took the folded fabric.

As they stepped out onto the bustling square, Eliza tucked the royal blue fabric under her arm as she walked alongside Ann.

"I'm telling you, Eliza, he has his eyes on you," Ann said, her eyes sparkling with mischief as she nudged her friend.

Eliza offered a faint smile, her thoughts far from the square, drifting to the memory of a fiddle's melody and a gentle hand guiding hers. She remained silent, her hazel eyes distant, the weight of the Nashville dinner pressing against her heart.

Ann's enthusiasm undimmed, she pressed on. "We should go to church tonight…" she said, her tone suggestive, a sly grin playing on her lips.

Eliza shook her head, a quiet laugh escaping her lips, the sound light but tinged with reluctance. "How about we go to the City Hotel and get some lunch instead?" she said, steering the conversation away from Elmore's upcoming performance.

Ann nodded eagerly, her excitement shifting to the prospect of a meal. "Perfect!" she said, as the two friends turned toward a hotel a few doors down.

An hour later, Elmore stood at the counter of the store, slowly gathering his fiddle case and jacket. Thomas Boyers leaned against a shelf, his face creased with a knowing gaze as he watched the younger man, his arms crossed casually.

"You're looking like you've got something on your mind, Elmore," Thomas said softly, his voice gentle but probing.

Elmore glanced up, surprised. "It's nothing, just… something I've been thinking about," he said, his tone guarded, a flush creeping up his neck.

Thomas chuckled, studying him with a fatherly warmth. "I can see it in your eyes. You've got a thing for Eliza, don't you?"

Elmore froze, taken aback, then sighed, his shoulders sagging as he looked his boss in the eye. "I reckon I do," he said quietly.

Thomas sighed, his tone soft but firm, a mix of sympathy and pragmatism. "I figured as much," he said. "But, Elmore… you know better than most how this town works. People talk. And folks already know the Governor's got his eye on her. You're not the only one drawn to her, son."

Elmore's jaw tightened. "I know," he said quietly. "It's not like I can do anything about it."

Thomas smiled sadly, stepping closer, his voice steady. "It ain't about what you can or can't do," he said. "It's about knowing where you stand. Sam Houston is a powerful man. He's got the ear of Andrew Jackson! And he's not some fool who won't fight for what he wants."

He paused, leaning in, his voice softening further. "You've been through enough in your life, Elmore," he said. "Losing your momma and daddy as a boy to becoming one of the finest musicians in Tennessee. I admire you… but you can't let yourself fall into a battle you know you can't win. Not over her. Not with him in the way."

Looking down at the floor, the weight of Thomas' words settled over Elmore. His fingers tightened on his jacket, his thoughts a tangle of longing and resignation. After a long pause, he straightened, pulling on his jacket with a grim resolve. "Thanks, Mr. Boyers," he said. "I appreciate it."

Thomas nodded, his eyes a mixture of concern and hope. "Take care of yourself, Elmore," he said. "I'll see you in the morning."

With his fiddle case in hand, Elmore walked out the door, his steps heavy.

◆ ◆ ◆ ◆ ◆ ◆

A block away, Eliza Allen and Ann Boyers stepped out of the City Hotel, their bubbly laughter lighting up the square like a melody. Ann patted her stomach contentedly, her blonde curls bouncing as she grinned.

Eliza's eyes sparkled with mischief, her usual reserve softened by a good lunch. "How many pieces of pie was that?" she teased. "Three? Four? Was it five?"

Ann's grin widened, her tone defensive but playful. "Three, but who's counting?" she said, her fan snapping open with a flourish. "I needed it. You know how much I love Mrs. Sindle's apple pie."

Eliza chuckled, shaking her head. "You're going to need a nap after that," she said, her laughter brightening the bustling street.

Ann nudged her, her grin undimmed. "Well, now

that I'm full, I need to run back to Daddy's store," she said. "You're heading home?"

Eliza nodded, adjusting the bundle of royal blue fabric under her arm. "Yes, mother wants to put my dress together tonight," she said.

As they walked down the street, Eliza's eyes caught a familiar figure emerging from Main Street. Elmore, tall and lean, carried his fiddle case, his dark hair slightly tousled from the day's work. He noticed her almost immediately, a faint smile tugging at the corner of his lips, his eyes brightening with a quiet warmth.

"Afternoon, Eliza," he called out softly, his voice carrying over the square's clamor.

Eliza's face softened, a warm smile curving her lips. "Afternoon, Elmore," she said, a spark of curiosity in her hazel eyes.

Ann, with a sly wink, gave Eliza a quick nudge before peeling off toward her father, who stood by the store's front door. Eliza turned her attention to Elmore, a little more open now, as if the fiddle lesson in the store had loosened a thread of her reserve.

Elmore gestured to the street ahead, his posture relaxed but hopeful. "I was about to grab a bite," he said. "Would you like to join me?"

Shaking her head, Eliza smiled gently. "Ann and I just ate," she said. "You're welcome to walk me home, though."

Elmore's eyes widened slightly, surprised but pleased, a quiet joy lighting up his face. "I'd like that," he said.

They began slowly walking down the street together, the square's bustle fading into a soft hum. The royal blue fabric felt heavier in Eliza's arms, a silent reminder of the governor's dinner, but Elmore's presence was a counterpoint, steady and unassuming.

After a pause, Elmore glanced at her, his voice quiet but curious. "You've been keeping busy?" he asked.

Eliza nodded. "Always, it seems," she said. "Lots to do at home. My mother's expecting me to go to a dinner for the Governor tomorrow."

Elmore raised an eyebrow, his expression changing slightly. "The Governor, huh?" he said. "I met him at the dance. He's very, uh, friendly."

Eliza shifted uncomfortably, her smile light but strained, the weight of Sam's charm and her parents' expectations pressing against her. "It's not like I have much of a choice in the matter," she said softly, her voice tinged with resignation.

They continued walking in silence for a moment, the tension easing as Eliza's smile returned, a playful glint in her eyes. "So, guess how many pieces of pie Ann ate with lunch?" she said, teasing, a smirk tugging at her lips.

Elmore laughed, breaking the quiet between them. "Knowing her?" he said, chuckling. "I'd say two, maybe three?"

Eliza grinned, her laughter bubbling up. "She said it was three, but I counted four!" she said, her voice bright with amusement.

Elmore's smile widened, his eyes crinkling with disbelief. "Four?!" he said, his laughter joining hers, a shared moment that felt as natural as the sunlight warming their path.

They laughed together, their steps slowing as they approached Allendale, its grand facade looming at the end of the square.

The Allendale front porch had white columns that framed a view of the quiet street. Eliza paused at the door, the royal blue fabric for her dress still tucked under her arm, her dark hair catching the afternoon light. She turned toward Elmore, who stood with his fiddle case in hand, his lean frame relaxed but his eyes bright with the warmth of their shared laughter. "Would you like to come in for a little while?" she asked softly.

Elmore smiled, a quiet joy softening his features. "I'd like that," he said, following her inside.

They settled on a cushioned settee in the parlor, the grand room softened by the golden light streaming through lace curtains. The air was filled with the light laughter from their earlier conversation about Ann's pie and small-town gossip. Their shoulders brushed slightly as they laughed, Eliza's eyes sparkling with amusement.

Eliza reached for the fiddle case in Elmore's lap, a playful twinkle in her eyes, and he tried to snatch it back, his grin matching hers. Their hands met, fingers brushing, as they shared a smile and a quiet connection.

The sound of footsteps approaching the parlor shattered the moment. They quickly pulled their hands apart, their smiles fading as Laetitia Allen entered, her stately figure framed in the doorway. Her eyes widened slightly, surprised to see Elmore, her expression shifting to one of polite scrutiny. "Oh!" she said, her voice bright but edged with curiosity. "Good afternoon."

Eliza's grin returned, her voice warm as she gestured to Elmore. "Mother, this is Elmore," she said. "He works at the store with Ann's father."

Laetitia studied the young man, her eyes sizing him up, her lips pursed as if weighing his presence in her parlor. Elmore furrowed his brow, puzzled by her scrutiny. "Uh, ma'am, I weighed the beans for you when you came by last week," he said, his voice polite but tinged with a hint of defensiveness.

Laetitia smiled politely, though her eyes betrayed a lack of enthusiasm. "Oh, yes…" she said, her tone courteous but distant. "It's nice to see you."

Elmore smiled, but he sensed her disapproval, his posture stiffening slightly under her watchful eye. Laetitia's attention shifted to Eliza, her frown deepening as she noticed the fabric on the table. "Eliza, dear, do you have the fabric I asked for?" she said, her voice firm. "We need to get started on your dress."

Eliza started to stand, her hand subconsciously brushing her dress as if to smooth it, her eyes holding on to Elmore, not quite ready for the visit to end. "Yes, Momma, I have it right here," she said, sighing as she reached for the fabric.

Laetitia looked at Elmore with a smile that was both courteous and dismissive, her posture signaling it was time for him to go. "Good," she said, motioning to the fabric. "We need to work on it, so it is ready for the dinner with Governor Houston tomorrow."

Elmore stood, nodding, his composure steady but his eyes betraying a hint of disappointment. "It's alright," he said. "I really should be going. Got some things to do at the church."

He gave Eliza a quick, almost reluctant smile. Eliza looked him in the eye, her voice gentle. "Thank you for walking me home."

Elmore tried to keep his tone upbeat, though a hint of regret seeped through. "I'll see you soon," he said, heading toward the door, his shoulders slumping slightly as he stepped out into the afternoon light.

As the door shut behind him, Eliza turned to her mother, her irritation building, a spark of defiance in her eyes. Laetitia cleared her throat. "Come along," she said. "Let's work on the dress. We don't have a lot of time…"

Eliza's jaw tightened, her frustration spilling over. "I'm not in a rush, Momma," she said sharply, her voice coiled with quiet menace.

Laetitia ignored her tone. "You know how important this dinner is, don't you?" she said firmly. "It could mean everything for your future. Sam Houston is not someone you let slip through your fingers."

Eliza's eyes flashed, her voice rising with frustration. "Momma, Elmore plays the…" she began, her words a desperate attempt to shift the conversation.

Laetitia cut her off sharply. "Governor Houston is a powerful man, Eliza," she said. "Think about it. He could offer you a life beyond anyone in this town can give you."

Eliza bit her lip, her frustration building into a wall of emotion she couldn't fully express. She picked up the fabric, her fingers shaking slightly as she folded it again. Laetitia walked away, her footsteps fading into the house, leaving Eliza standing in the parlor, the weight of her mother's words pressing against her chest like a stone.

♦ ♦ ♦ ♦ ♦ ♦

Laetitia's bedroom was a sanctuary of order, its polished mahogany furniture and lace-trimmed curtains bathed in the soft glow of oil lamps. A large mirror stood in one corner, reflecting the royal blue fabric draped across a table. Eliza stood in the center, her posture rigid, her arms outstretched as Laetitia pinned the fabric against her, the faint rustle of cloth the only sound breaking the oppressive silence. The air was thick with the scent of lavender, but it did little to ease the tension coiling in Eliza's chest.

Laetitia moved with practiced precision, her fingers deft as she measured the fabric along Eliza's shoulders, her lips curved in a determined smile. Her dark hair was pinned neatly, her dress impeccable, but her eyes darted to Eliza's face, seeking to break the ice. "This blue will look stunning on you," she said, her voice bright, almost coaxing, as she adjusted a pin. "It'll catch every eye in Nashville."

Eliza's jaw tightened, her hazel eyes fixed on the mirror, staring past her own reflection to some distant point. She didn't respond, her silence a wall, her anger simmering from their earlier clash in the parlor. The memory of Elmore's hasty departure, Laetitia's dismissive tone, and the relentless push toward Sam Houston's world burned within her, each pin a prick against her resolve.

Laetitia, undeterred, smoothed the fabric along Eliza's waist, her movements brisk but gentle. "Mrs. Donelson was telling me about the governor's last speech," she said, her tone conversational, as if unaware of the storm brewing in her daughter. "Such a commanding presence. You'll see it tomorrow, dear, how he lights up a room."

Eliza's fingers twitched at her sides, her teeth grinding. She shifted slightly, her shoulder stiffening under Laetitia's touch, but she said nothing, her silence louder than any words. The royal blue fabric felt like a chain, each measurement a step toward a future she didn't choose.

Laetitia paused, her hands hovering over the fabric, her smile faltering as she glanced at Eliza's stony expression. "You'll be the belle of the dinner," she said, her voice softer now, almost pleading, as she pinned the hem. "Think of the people you will meet."

Eliza looked at her mother's reflection, a tinge of defiance in her eyes, but she bit back the words that rose in her throat. "I cannot wait, Mother," she muttered, her tone simmering below the surface, the barest acknowledgment before her eyes returned to the mirror.

Laetitia sighed, a faint crease forming on her brow, but she resumed her work, her fingers moving faster now, as if to outpace the silence. She stepped back, surveying the draped fabric, her smile returning with forced brightness. "Perfect," she said, more to herself than Eliza, as she gathered her pins. "We'll have this ready by morning."

Lowering her arms, the fabric slid slightly, Eliza's posture was stiff as she stepped away from the center of the room. She didn't look at her mother. Laetitia turned to the table, humming softly, oblivious to the storm raging in her daughter's silence.

A Night in Nashville

June 15, 1828, Gallatin, Tennessee

The carriage stopped in downtown Nashville, its wheels crunching on the dirt street amid the evening bustle. Gaslights shimmered, casting a golden glow over the sidewalks, where men in top hats and women in fine silks moved with purpose. Eliza sat in her new royal blue dress, its modest elegance accentuating her poised but nervous demeanor. The dress, stitched with her mother's expectations, felt awkward and uncomfortable against her skin, a reminder of the role she was expected to play.

Congressman Robert Allen stepped out first, his well-tailored coat and confident stride marking him as a man at ease in this world. He turned, offering his hand to his niece with a warm smile. "You look lovely, my dear," he said affectionately as he helped her down from the carriage.

Eliza's feet touched the ground, but her eyes widened, her breath catching as she took in the city's vibrancy. Carriages clattered past, their horses snorting; and the grand facades of buildings stood imposingly. She stood frozen, like a startled doe in the brush, her hands clutching her shawl, the weight of Nashville's grandeur pressing against her.

Noticing her unease, Robert's smile softened as he placed a reassuring hand on her arm. "Breathe, Eliza," he said softly. "Enjoy yourself tonight. This is a chance to meet new people. But be cautious around Mrs. Eaton. The last time I saw her, she started laughing and accidentally spit chewing tobacco all over my new shoes." Eliza looked at him, unsure if he was joking. Robert deadpanned, slowly nodding his head, his eyes twinkling with mischief. A snicker escaped Eliza, her hand flying to cover her mouth, the tension in her shoulders easing as his humor broke through her nerves.

Eliza nodded, her hazel eyes darting from the bustling street to her uncle's steady gaze. He leaned closer, his voice lowering with a conspiratorial warmth. "If you need me, I'm right here," he said. "I know your mother's putting pressure on you, but I want you to have fun. Be yourself."

He reached into his coat and pulled out a small silver flask. He took a quick drink, the sharp scent of whiskey cutting through the night air, then offered it to her, his grin widening. Eliza's eyes opened wide, disbelief flashing across her face, her lips parting in surprise. After a moment, a chuckle escaped her as she took the flask.

She raised it to her lips, the whiskey burning as it slid down her throat, her face contorting in a grimace that drew a hearty laugh from Robert. "Oh, my!" she gasped, coughing lightly, her cheeks flushing as she handed the flask back.

Robert's laughter softened, his eyes crinkling with affection. Eliza stepped closer, rising on her toes to kiss his cheek, her voice warm with gratitude. "Thank you, Uncle," she said, her smile genuine, a spark of courage kindled by his easy support.

The parlor was alive with conversation, its walls adorned with rich tapestries and portraits. Lawmakers, businessmen, and their wives sipped from crystal glasses, nibbling hors d'oeuvres passed by servants. Laughter and debate filled the room, a tapestry of ambition and influence.

Standing near the fireplace, Sam Houston's tall frame commanded attention, his deep laugh resonating as he held court with a group of well-dressed men. His tailored coat and charismatic grin made him the room's center, a star in his element. He spotted Eliza across the crowd, his eyes lighting with recognition, and immediately made his way toward her.

"Miss Eliza, you look radiant this evening."

Eliza curtsied politely, her movements graceful despite the flutter in her chest. "Governor Houston, thank you," she said, her voice steady but soft, her eyes meeting his briefly before looking to the crowd.

Sam grinned, undeterred. "I told you, call me Sam." He turned to the group of men he'd been speaking with, gesturing for one to join him. "There's someone I'd like you to meet."

A dashing young politician stepped forward. "Miss Eliza Allen, this is Congressman James Polk from Maury County," Sam said proudly.

Polk bowed slightly. "It's a pleasure to meet you, Miss Allen," he said. "Your uncle is a fine man."

Eliza nodded her head, her smile polite but reserved. "Thank you, Congressman," she said. "The pleasure is mine."

Before she could catch her breath, Willoughby Williams, a dapper but portly gentleman, waddled over, his affable grin lighting his round face. "Is this the young lady you've been telling me about?" he asked, his voice booming with enthusiasm.

Sam beamed, his pride evident. "Dear, this is Sheriff Williams."

Eliza maintained a polite smile, her demeanor

composed while her eyes revealed a hint of being overwhelmed. The parlor's chatter swelled, a tide of voices and faces that threatened to sweep her away, as she stood in the governor's orbit, a guest in a world that dazzled but felt far from her own.

Moments later, she found refuge near the edge of the room, her royal blue dress pooling gracefully around her as she sat with a small glass of water in hand. She sipped slowly, eyes scanning the sea of strangers, her posture carefully poised.

A sudden commotion rippled through the crowd — a shift in energy like wind through tall grass. A murmur rose, scattering the rhythm of conversation and dance.

"He's here!" someone called out, the voice bright with anticipation.

Eliza's head turned, her brow furrowing as a low murmur filled the ballroom, the crowd's attention shifting toward the entrance. All eyes turned as Andrew Jackson, the President of the United States, strode into the room, his presence commanding and electrifying. His lean frame, clad in a tailored black coat, moved with a soldier's confidence, his sharp eyes scanning the room as the crowd parted before him. He greeted those closest with hearty handshakes and smiles, his voice booming with warmth, a legend in motion.

Sam leaned down to Eliza, his breath warm against her ear. "Would you like to meet the General?" he asked eagerly, his eyes alight with pride.

Eliza hesitated, her heart racing, overwhelmed by the moment, but she nodded, her resolve steadying. Sam offered his hand, his grip firm and reassuring, and they wove through the crowd, the sea of faces blurring as they approached the President.

"General Jackson, may I present Miss Eliza Allen," Sam said, his voice carrying over the murmur, his posture proud. "She is the niece of Congressman Allen."

Jackson turned, his sharp eyes softening as he took in Eliza, his weathered face creasing with a warm smile. "Miss Allen, a pleasure," he said, his voice rich with Southern cadence. "Your uncle—he's a firebrand, a true asset to the party."

Eliza curtsied, her movements graceful, her voice steady despite the nerves fluttering in her chest. "The honor is mine, Mr. President," she said, her eyes meeting his briefly before lowering in respect.

Jackson chuckled, clearly amused, and began a light-hearted conversation, his stories laced with both humor and authority. Just as he spoke, a loud, confident woman approached, her presence impossible to ignore. She walked arm in arm with a man in a suit, and their arrival turned heads. Her dark hair was elegantly swept up, and her long gown demanded attention, but it was her defiant demeanor that truly stood out. Jackson gestured toward them, his smile widening. "Miss Allen, Senator John Eaton and his wife, Peggy," he said with warmth.

Peggy began to speak but a small dribble of tobacco juice ran down the side of her mouth. Eliza's eyes widened slightly, Robert's earlier warning running through her mind, a mix of amusement and disbelief stirring within her. Jackson caught the moment, his lips twitching with a tickled smile, his eyes darting to Eliza and Sam with a conspiratorial glint. Sam suppressed a chuckle, his hand tightening briefly on Eliza's arm.

The President excused himself, patting Sam on the shoulder with a knowing nod before moving on, his presence pulling the crowd's attention with him like a tide. Eliza stood rooted, her breath shallow, caught between awe and disorientation. The encounter had left her lightheaded, the ballroom's whirl seeming to spin faster around her, the chatter and movement blurring into a dizzying blur of silk, laughter, and perfume.

Sensing her unease, Sam leaned in gently. Without a word, he offered his arm, and together they slipped from the glow and noise of the party into the cooler calm of the night. The sounds of the ballroom faded behind them, replaced by the soft hum of Nashville's dirt streets and the distant hush of the river.

They strolled along the wharf by the Cumberland, where lanterns shone against the water's surface, casting golden ribbons that danced atop the silver sheen of moonlight. The distant clatter of riverboats docking, men shouting over crates and chains, provided a steady rhythm to the quiet between them.

Sam said little at first, his hands folded behind his back, the tail of his coat catching the lantern glow as he walked. There was a steadiness to him, as if he were made for nights like this—quiet, thoughtful, a man carrying more than he let on.

"What a night, wouldn't you agree?" he said, his voice warm, a smile playing on his lips as he glanced at her.

Eliza nodded, her royal blue dress brushing the dusty street. "It's been… remarkable," she said, her voice soft, her thoughts still reeling from the ballroom's dazzle and Jackson's towering presence.

They stopped at the edge of the wharf. A steamboat moved slowly across the water, its paddlewheel slicing the river into waves that lapped gently against the dock. Lanterns from the ship shimmered like stars scattered across the water.

Sam turned toward her. His expression shifted—more serious now, stripped of the playful charm he'd worn all evening. His gaze found hers, steady and searching.

"Miss Eliza," he said softly, "I must confess something to you."

Turning to him, Eliza's heart beat faster, a bit of unease stirring within her. She remained silent, her gaze steady but guarded, unsure where his words would lead.

"I've been thinking a great deal about my future," Sam continued, his tone deliberate. "About Tennessee's future."

Eliza listened, her breath shallow, the river's quiet lapping a counterpoint to the tension building in her chest. Sam turned to face her fully, his eyes locking onto hers, his ambition a palpable force. "The people of Tennessee need a first lady," he said. "They deserve a first lady…"

He paused, his gaze softening but unwavering. "Would you consider being the First Lady of Tennessee?" he asked, his voice steady, the question hanging in the air like a challenge.

Eliza's breath caught, her eyes widening as the weight of his words settled over her. "Governor, I… I don't know what to say," she said, her voice trembling slightly, her thoughts racing in a whirlwind of awe and apprehension.

Smiling warmly, Sam stepped closer, his presence enveloping. "And who knows—after the General completes his second term in Washington, I might find myself in the Executive Mansion."

His words hung in the air. A promise, a plan, a world just out of reach.

He tilted his head, watching her closely. "Could you see that life for yourself?" he asked.

Eliza turned back to the river, her hands tightening on her shawl, her thoughts a tumult of conflicting desires. The fairy tale was intoxicating—balls, power, a name that echoed across the nation—but its weight felt heavy on her shoulders, a gilded cage that clashed with the memory of a fiddle's melody and a quiet walk home. Sam watched her carefully as the river's ripples carried her silence into the night.

Present Day

Lying in bed, Eliza sighed, her gaze distant, as if she could still see the Cumberland River's ripples under Nashville's moonlight. The firelight danced across her lined face, catching the twinkle in her eyes. Susie leaned closer, her breath held, the letter still in her hands, her voice barely above a whisper. "He asked you to marry him?" she asked, her eyes searching her mother's for the answer to a question that felt like destiny.

Eliza's lips curled into a faint, bittersweet smile, the kind that held both joy and sorrow in its curve. "He didn't quite ask," she said, her voice soft, threaded with the weight of memory. "But he made his intentions clear."

Susie's eyes widened, her voice trembling with anticipation. "What did you say?" she asked, leaning forward.

Eliza's eyes glistened, the firelight dancing in their depths as she looked toward the flames. "What else could I say?" she said, her voice a whisper. "He was the governor..."

Secrets Beneath the Stars

July 14, 1828, Gallatin, Tennessee

The sun dipped below the horizon, painting the Gallatin town square in a warm, amber glow, the dirt streets soft under the fading light. Eliza Allen drove a horse-drawn buggy, the steady clop of hooves a rhythmic heartbeat in the still evening. A soft breeze stirred the ribbons on her bonnet, brushing against her cheek like a whisper of doubt. Her royal blue dress, now a symbol of Sam's dazzling world, lay folded at home, as did the memory of his voice by the river, asking her to be Tennessee's First Lady.

The square was quieter than usual, its usual bustle softened to a gentle hum.

Suddenly, the clear, inviting chime of church bells rang through the air. Eliza's head turned, her hazel eyes narrowing as she traced the sound to the small church at the square's edge. Through the twilight, she saw a stream of people walking toward it, their figures silhouetted against the glow of lanterns hanging at the church doors, their murmurs a soft undercurrent of community.

Her eyes caught a familiar figure among them—Elmore, dressed neatly in a pressed shirt and trousers, his fiddle case swinging at his side. He walked alone, his lean frame moving with a quiet purpose. Eliza's breath hitched, her fingers tightening on the reins as she watched him disappear into the church.

She stared at the reins, her heart torn between Sam's ambition and Elmore's melody. She glanced toward the street leading home, where her mother's expectations and Sam's proposal waited, then back to the church, where a simpler truth beckoned. She exhaled deeply as she made her decision.

With a gentle tug, she guided the buggy back around, the horse snorting as it obeyed, the wheels creaking as they turned toward the church.

Eliza pulled the buggy to a stop just outside the churchyard, careful to remain unnoticed in the shadows. She climbed down, smoothing her dress with trembling hands. The church's illuminated windows glowed like beacons. Faint laughter and warm greetings floated toward her, mingling with the hum of conversation, a community gathered in shared faith and song.

She hesitated, her heart pounding, then straightened her back, her resolve firming like a river finding its course. With quiet steps, she walked toward the church doors, slipping inside as the music began.

The modest church was dimly lit by lanterns, their glimmering light dancing across the wooden pews. The air hummed with the soulful strains of a fiddle, Elmore standing near the pulpit, his bow gliding across the strings in a heartfelt hymn. His eyes were half-closed, his face alight with the music's quiet power.

Slipping into the back row, Eliza pulled her bonnet low, her face partially hidden in the shadows. She sat alone, her hands folded tightly in her lap, her eyes fixed on Elmore, her heart heavy with the weight of Nashville's dazzle and the proposal that had followed. The hymn wrapped around her, its melody stirring memories of a fiddle lesson, a walk home, laughter in the parlor when the world felt small and true.

Elmore glanced up from his playing, his eyes catching hers. His fingers faltered for a brief moment, the bow hesitating on the strings, a hint of surprise crossing his face. He quickly recovered, his gaze lingering as he finished the piece, the final note fading into a reverent silence.

After the pastor made some announcements, Eliza slipped out the back, her footsteps light as she moved toward the edge of the churchyard, her heart racing with the need to escape unnoticed.

"Eliza!" Elmore's voice called, soft but urgent, cutting through the night.

She froze, her breath catching, her hands tightening on her shawl. Slowly, she turned to see him hurrying toward her, his fiddle case still in hand, his face lit by the faint glow of a nearby lantern. "You came to hear me play?" he asked, his voice trembling with hope, his eyes searching hers.

Eliza nodded, her voice unsteady, a quiver betraying the storm within her. "You play beautifully, Elmore," she said, her words soft but earnest. "I… I wanted to hear it again."

Elmore smiled faintly, but a sadness shadowed his eyes, as if he sensed the weight she carried. "Thank you," he said. "It means a lot that you came."

He gestured to a bench in the adjoining graveyard, its wood silvered by moonlight. "Would you like to sit for a while?" he asked.

Eliza hesitated, then nodded, her heart pulling her toward him despite the chaos within. They walked through the grave markers, and sat on the bench, the faint chirp of crickets filling the silence.

Elmore watched as Eliza gazed up at the stars, his eyes tracing the curve of her cheek, the tension in her shoulders. He hesitated and then finally spoke. "Is it true?" he asked, the words laden with dread.

Eliza turned to him, her brow knitting. "What?" she asked, her voice soft, uncertain.

Elmore's gaze dropped. "Are you engaged to the governor?" he asked.

Her composure shattered, tears welling in her eyes as she nodded. "Yes," she said quietly.

She looked away, shame coloring her cheeks, her tears catching the moonlight. "It's what my parents want," she said, her words barely audible. "It's what he wants."

Elmore leaned back, his face shadowed but etched with anguish. "And what do you want?" he asked, his voice raw, a plea for the truth she hid even from herself.

Eliza didn't answer immediately, her tears falling silently, her eyes fixed on the ground. "I don't know," she whispered, the words a confession, fragile and true.

Elmore exhaled deeply, his voice shaking, his heart laid bare. "I have feelings for you, Eliza," he said, the admission a quiet thunder in the stillness, his eyes searching hers for a spark of hope.

Looking at him, Eliza's tears fell freely, her heart aching with the truth she couldn't deny. "Elmore…" she began, her voice trembling, a plea and a warning in one.

He pressed on, his words spilling out. "But I can't get in the way of the governor's marriage," he said. "I wouldn't do that to you — or to him."

He stood abruptly, the fiddle case swinging at his side, his posture rigid with resolve. "You deserve the life he can give you," Elmore said, his voice strained. "A big house, fancy dinners, a name that commands respect. I… I couldn't give you any of that."

He turned to leave, his steps slow and reluctant,

each one a wound. Eliza's heart lurched, a desperate need rising within her. "Elmore, wait!" she cried, rising from the bench, her voice cracking as she ran after him, grabbing his arm.

Before he could protest, she kissed him deeply, her hands framing his face, her desperation pouring into the moment, a fleeting defiance against the world that sought to claim her. The kiss was fire and sadness, a promise of what could have been, her tears mingling with his breath.

Elmore pulled away gently, his face filled with sorrow, his hands trembling as he touched her arms. "You can't do this," he said, his voice breaking. "You're going to be his wife."

Eliza's eyes blazed with a fierce longing, her voice raw. "I'd like to be with you," she said, the words a confession she hadn't dared speak until now, her heart laid bare under the starry sky.

Elmore shook his head, his anguish palpable, his voice cracking with the weight of truth. "You deserve more than what I could ever give you," he said. "And you… you don't belong in my world."

He placed his hand lightly on her shoulder, a final, tender gesture, his eyes glistening with unshed tears. "God bless you and your husband, Eliza," he said, his voice a whisper. "I wish you well."

He stepped back, his eyes staying on her one last time, a silent goodbye etched in the lines of his face. Then he turned, walking away.

Standing motionless, the weight of Elmore's words pressing heavily on Eliza's chest, her tears streaming down her face. She looked up at the stars, their cold light offering no answers, her mind a whirlwind of conflicting emotions—caught between the safety and grandeur of a life with Sam Houston and the quiet, simple life with Elmore, a life that felt like home but slipped through her fingers like sand.

Present Day

The bedroom was bathed in the soft glow of firelight, its crackling the only sound as Eliza's voice trembled with the weight of her memories. Susie sat beside her, leaning in intently, her young face etched with awe and curiosity, the letter in her hands a tether to the past.

Eliza sighed. "That night, I felt torn in two," she said, her voice soft, laced with a longing that time hadn't dulled. "As a girl I dreamed of fairy tales, of castles and grand titles… but life isn't a fairy tale."

She paused, her eyes glistening, the fire's warmth a faint comfort against the chill of regret. "I didn't love Sam," she said, the confession sharp and raw. "Not really. I admired him, respected him… but love? No."

Susie gently placed a hand on her mother's, her touch a quiet anchor. "Then why did you agree to marry him?" she asked, her voice barely above a whisper, her eyes searching for the truth behind the choice.

Eliza exhaled deeply, her shoulders sinking under the weight of the question, her fingers tightening briefly on the quilt. "Because I thought it was what I was supposed to do," she said. "For my family, for myself…"

Her lips pressed together, her eyes glistening as the memory rose, vivid and unrelenting. "But Elmore…" she said, his name a soft breath, a melody she'd carried in her heart. "There was something about him. A kindness, a simplicity… something I'd never known but desperately wanted."

Susie tilted her head, her voice quiet but insistent, a spark of hope in her eyes. "Did you love him?" she asked, the question hanging like a star in the dimness.

Eliza closed her eyes, her answer caught between honesty and regret, her face softening with the weight of a truth she'd held close. "I don't know if it was love," she said, her voice catching. "Not yet. But I felt something I couldn't name. A connection. A longing to know him better."

Her voice trembled, and she steadied herself. "And I knew… I couldn't," she said, her words a quiet surrender. "Not with the path I had chosen."

The fire popped softly, filling the weighted silence that followed.

Araby's Daughter

January 22, 1829, Gallatin, Tennessee

The grand Allen mansion hummed with life, its halls alive with chatter and clattering preparations spilling through the open window of Eliza's bedroom.

Before the mirror, Eliza stood still as Ann and two bridesmaids flitted around her, pinning and adjusting folds of lace and satin. Her reflection gleamed — poised, radiant — but her hazel eyes told another story, distant and uncertain.

"You look like a queen," Ann chirped, her smile radiant as she pinned back a stray lock of Eliza's hair.

Eliza managed a faint smile.

Ann moved to the window, snapping open her fan. "The whole town must be here! Look, there's Mrs. Trousdale!" she exclaimed, leaning out.

Eliza barely heard her, her gaze rooted to her own reflection — the face of a girl about to become someone else's idea of a wife.

Ann gasped. "And look — Elmore's here! He brought his fiddle!"

Eliza froze. She drifted to the window, her skirts whispering against the floor.

Down below, the musicians unloaded their instruments from a wagon. Among them, Elmore stood, somber in his Sunday best, his fiddle case swinging loosely at his side.

For a heartbeat, their eyes almost met. Eliza's breath caught. She stepped back quickly, hands fluttering to her dress, her heart hammering against her ribs.

Ann turned, teasing, "The Governor is waiting, Eliza — don't swoon over the fiddle player now."

Eliza forced a laugh. "Don't be ridiculous," she said lightly, smoothing her skirt with trembling fingers.

The door swung open. Laetitia Allen entered, regal and proud.

"Eliza, darling, it's time," she said, extending a steadying hand.

The bridesmaids flurried around her, adjusting lace and satin.

"You're about to become Mrs. Sam Houston," Laetitia said warmly. "The whole state will remember this day."

Eliza let herself be led from the room. Beneath her serene exterior, her heart carried only the echo of a fiddle's song.

◆ ◆ ◆ ◆ ◆ ◆

In a quiet spare bedroom down the hall, the air was warm with the scent of polished wood and the faint tang of cigar smoke. A tall mirror stood in one corner, reflecting the figures of three men preparing for the day's ceremony. Sam Houston adjusted his finely tailored coat, his fingers smoothing the fabric as he studied his reflection, his face alight with a confident smile, the smooth politician ready to claim his bride.

John Allen, Eliza's father, stood nearby, his salt and pepper hair neatly combed, his suit impeccable, his eyes bright with pride as he fastened his cufflinks. "I couldn't be happier to have the governor of Tennessee as my son-in-law," he said, his voice rich with satisfaction, a broad grin spreading across his face as he clapped Sam on the shoulder.

Sam chuckled, a deep, warm sound that filled the room, his reflection catching the light as he turned from the mirror. "I'm honored, John," he said, his tone genial, his eyes twinkling with the weight of the moment.

Robert Allen, the congressman, stood a step back, his expression more reserved, his face etched with a quiet concern that tempered his smile. He stepped forward, his hand extended to Sam, his grip firm but measured. "Welcome to the family, Sam," he said, his voice steady but lacking John's fervor, a shadow of caution in his eyes.

Sam shook his hand, his smile unwavering, but Robert held his gaze, his tone softening with a fatherly weight. "Be patient with her," he said, leaning in, deliberate. "I love her dearly, but she's still a child in many ways. She may not be ready for all the pressure that's about to be placed upon her."

Sam nodded, his expression sobering, his hand tightening briefly on Robert's. "I will honor her and protect her, always," he said, his voice firm, a vow that carried the weight of his ambition and his heart.

Robert's eyes lingered on Sam's, a flicker of hope mingling with his concern, before he stepped back, the room settling into a quiet moment of shared purpose, the weight of the day pressing gently against them all.

◆ ◆ ◆ ◆ ◆ ◆

The Allen mansion's parlor was a vision of elegance, transformed into a picturesque setting for the wedding, its polished floors adorned with garlands of fresh roses and lilies, their scent mingling with the warmth of morning light. Chairs were arranged in neat rows, filled with guests in fine dresses and suits, their murmurs a soft hum of anticipation, the air buzzing with excitement that would echo across Tennessee. At the rear, a small wooden platform served as the altar, where William Hume, a distinguished elderly minister, stood ready.

Soft music floated through the air, a tender melody played by the musicians seated near the platform. Elmore sat slightly apart, his head bowed, his bow gliding steadily over his fiddle's strings, the notes melancholic and hauntingly beautiful, each one a whisper of sorrow. His dark hair fell across his brow, his expression distant, as if the music were his only shield against the day's pain.

The door opened, and Eliza stepped out, her arm linked with her father, John Allen, his proud posture a contrast to her quiet reserve. Her wedding dress was exquisite, layers of white lace and satin cascading around her. Her face was calm, almost too calm, a mask that hid the storm within her heart. She took a hesitant step forward, her eyes immediately drawn to Elmore, his bowed head a silent wound she couldn't touch.

Elmore refused to look at her, his focus fixed on his fiddle, his fingers steady but his expression tight, as if each note were a farewell. The music shifted, the melody slowing into a familiar, brooding tune that tugged at Eliza's memory. Her brow furrowed, her steps hesitating as she tried to place it. Then it hit her — "Araby's Daughter," the song Elmore had played for her in the store's back room, now woven with a quiet grief that pierced her heart.

Eliza's mouth opened, a silent gasp as she glanced at Elmore. The guests rose, their smiles warm as they watched the reluctant bride approach, oblivious to the silent dialogue woven into the fiddle's strains. John led her down the aisle, but Eliza's thoughts were with the melody, its slow, haunting notes a mirror to her inner conflict.

Sam Houston stood at the altar, tall and resplendent in a sharp suit, his smile widening as he saw Eliza, his eyes alight with pride and certainty. She barely noticed, her attention caught between the altar and the faint strains of the fiddle.

When she reached the altar, Eliza's father placed her hand in Sam's, his touch warm but unfamiliar. Her hand trembled slightly, and Sam gave it a reassuring squeeze, his smile unwavering, as if he could will her doubts away. Reverend Hume stepped forward, his voice steady and warm.

"Dearly beloved, we are gathered here in the sight of God and this company to join together this man and this woman in holy matrimony…" he began, his words resonant in the hushed parlor.

Eliza's gaze shifted to the musicians, where the music had stopped, the silence stark and heavy. Elmore sat still, his fiddle resting in his lap, his head bowed, refusing to look up, his silence louder than any note he'd played. The minister's voice continued, a steady drone that blurred in Eliza's mind. "…to have and to hold, from this day forward, for better or for worse…"

Her heart raced, a tide of emotion rising within her, the urge to cry a pressure she fought to contain. Hume turned to the governor, his tone clear. "Sam Houston, do you take this woman to be your wedded wife?"

Sam's smile was radiant. "I do," he said firmly, his eyes locked on Eliza, as if she were the center of his world.

Hume turned to Eliza. "Eliza Allen, do you take this man to be your wedded husband?"

A tense silence fell over the crowd, the air thick with expectation. Eliza's breath caught, her eyes darting to Elmore, his stillness a quiet agony, his bowed head a refusal to witness her choice. She paused, her heart pounding, the weight of the moment pressing against her like a storm. She looked to the front row, where Laetitia sat, her mother's eyes glaring with unyielding expectation, sharp and unmerciful, a silent command that bore into her. Eliza exhaled, a shuddering breath that carried her resolve, her voice emerging barely above a whisper, fragile and strained. "I… I do," she said, the words a surrender she felt in her bones.

Hume nodded, his voice warm as he continued. "By the power vested in me, I now pronounce you husband and wife," he said, his words sealing her fate.

Sam grinned, lifting Eliza's veil with a tender touch, leaning in to kiss her. She tilted her head mechanically, her lips barely meeting his, her eyes glistening with unshed tears. The crowd erupted in claps and cheers, their joy a stark contrast to the aching in her heart.

Soft music resumed, a lighter tune that filled the parlor as guests rose from their seats, mingling and offering congratulations. Sam beamed, shaking hands and accepting pats on the back, his pride radiant. "She's beautiful, isn't she?" he said to a guest, his voice warm with affection.

Forcing a smile, Eliza nodded politely to well-wishers. She glanced at the musicians, Elmore in particular, his fiddle silent, his face shadowed by sorrow.

She turned to Sam abruptly, her voice sharp with need. "I need a moment, please," she said, her tone clipped.

Sam frowned, confusion clouding his smile, but he nodded. "Of course, my dear," he said, his voice gentle, though his eyes searched hers for answers she couldn't give.

Eliza gathered her dress, and walked briskly toward the hallway, her steps quickening as the parlor's noise faded behind her.

She broke into a run in the hallway, her wedding dress trailing behind her like a ghost. Tears spilled down her cheeks, hot and unrelenting, her sobs a silent cry for a life she hadn't chosen.

Bursting into her bedroom, Eliza slammed the door behind her. She leaned against it, her body trembling. Her hands clutched her veil, tearing it from her head with a desperate yank, the delicate fabric fluttering to the ground like a fallen dream. Tears still streaming down her cheeks, she sank against the door.

She lifted her hand, her eyes locking onto the gold wedding ring, its gleam a stark reminder of the vow she'd just made. Her fingers curled around it, tightening as if to pull it free, but she stopped, a shudder coursing through her, disbelief and despair warring within her.

The door creaked open, and Ann slipped inside, her bright demeanor faltering as she took in Eliza's fragile state, her eyes widening with concern. "Eliza? What's wrong?" she asked, her voice soft, urgent, as she crossed the room.

Eliza turned to face her, her eyes red and glistening, her voice raw with emotion. "I… I can't do this," she said, the words a confession.

Ann rushed to her side, taking her hands, her grip

warm but firm. "Eliza, you're just overwhelmed," she said reassuringly, though her brow furrowed with confusion. "It was a beautiful ceremony. Everything's perfect—"

"No, Ann, it's not," Eliza interrupted, her voice sharp, her tears rolling down her face. "None of this is right."

Ann's confusion deepened. "You don't mean that," she said, her voice gentle but insistent. "Sam Houston is a good man—powerful, respected. You'll have everything you've ever dreamed of."

Eliza shook her head. "That's just it," she said. "It's not what I dreamed of."

Ann hesitated, her gaze sharpening as she pieced together her friend's turmoil. "Is this about… Elmore?" she asked, her voice softening, cautious.

Eliza's breath hitched, her face turning away, her silence a confirmation she couldn't voice. Ann sighed, her expression tender as she sat beside Eliza on the edge of the bed, wrapping an arm around her shoulders. "I saw the way you looked at him earlier," she said, her voice a quiet acknowledgment of a truth they both knew.

Eliza sank into the bed, her hands trembling in her lap, her voice barely above a whisper. "He won't even look at me now," she said, her words heavy with loss, the memory of Elmore's bowed head cutting deeper than any vow.

Ann's grip tightened, her voice gentle but firm. "Eliza, he's just a fiddle player who works at a general store," she said. "What kind of life could you have with him?"

Eliza looked up, her expression fierce despite her tears, her eyes blazing with a longing she couldn't suppress. "A simple one," she said. "A real one."

Ann's face softened, her arm pulling Eliza closer, her voice a whisper of empathy. "Oh, Eliza…" she said, the words trailing into silence.

A gentle knock sounded at the door, breaking the quiet. Laetitia Allen stepped inside, poised and composed, her elegant gown a stark contrast to Eliza's disheveled state. Her eyes softened as she took in her daughter's tear-streaked face, but her posture remained regal. "Eliza, darling, the guests are waiting," she said, her voice warm but firm. "It's time to rejoin your husband."

Eliza inhaled sharply at the word "husband," but Laetitia stepped forward, smoothing the folds of Eliza's dress with a practiced hand, her smile gentle yet unyielding. "I am so proud of you," she said, her voice rich with conviction. "Come now, let's show them how radiant you look."

Eliza nodded faintly, her movements slow as she grabbed her crumpled veil, forcing herself to her feet, her tears drying but her heart still racing. Ann gave her an encouraging squeeze on the shoulder, her eyes warm with support, before slipping out behind Laetitia, leaving Eliza to gather the fragments of her composure.

After taking a deep breath, Eliza descended the grand staircase, her steps slow and deliberate. Her attention was drawn to the doorway where Sam Houston stood, his tall frame commanding as he spoke with the band members.

Sam's voice was jovial, his smile broad as he shook hands with the three musicians, pulling folded banknotes from his pocket and handing one to each. "Thank you, gentlemen," he said, his tone warm with gratitude. "Your music added just the right touch to the ceremony."

The first band member nodded, his grin wide. "Thank you, Governor," he said, pocketing the note with a respectful dip of his head.

Elmore stood slightly apart, his posture polite but tense, his eyes carefully avoiding Sam's gaze, his fiddle case a silent weight at his side. He accepted the payment last, his face shadowed by a quiet sorrow.

Sam's smiled as he looked at Elmore, his voice rich with admiration. "You've got real talent, young man," he said. "That fiddle of yours has a way of stirring the soul."

Elmore nodded respectfully. "Thank you, sir," he said, doing his best to remain composed.

As Sam clapped Elmore on the shoulder, both men turned, their eyes catching Eliza standing at the base of the staircase, her figure framed by the foyer's grandeur. The room seemed to quiet, the air charged as their eyes locked with hers, a moment suspended between worlds—Sam's bright ambition and Elmore's silent longing.

Sam's expression brightened, his admiration clear, his voice warm with pride. "There's my beautiful bride," he said, his smile radiant, his hand extending toward her as if to claim the future they'd vowed to share.

Elmore quickly looked away, stepping back with the other musicians, his figure retreating into the crowd's periphery. Eliza walked toward Sam, her face calm but her heart pounding, each step a battle between the life she'd chosen and the one she'd left behind.

That afternoon, the sun had started to dip lower, casting long shadows across the Allen mansion's sprawling yard, its golden light softened by the crisp chill that crept into the air. Guests lingered, their shawls pulled tighter against the winter breeze, their voices a warm hum as they exchanged congratulations with the newlyweds.

Sam Houston stood near the waiting carriage as he shook hands with ease, his voice carrying a practiced warmth that charmed those gathered around. "Thank you for coming," he said to a well-wisher, his smile broad, his presence as commanding as ever.

Eliza stood beside him, her hands clasped tightly in front of her, a thin shawl draped over her shoulders, its delicate weave doing little to shield her from the cold she barely noticed. Her smile was faint and fleeting, a fragile mask that took great effort to hold, her hazel eyes distant, as if searching for something beyond the crowd.

John Allen approached, his face alight with pride as he opened his arms to Eliza. "My dear girl," he said, his voice warm, pulling her into a gentle embrace. Eliza returned the hug, her smile slipping as she pressed her cold cheek to his shoulder.

Laetitia followed, her elegant gown rustling, her composure regal but her eyes softening with maternal pride. She enveloped Eliza in a tender hug, her hands smoothing her daughter's shawl. "I love you so much," she whispered.

John turned to Sam, extending his hand with a broad grin. "Governor, it's an honor," he said, his handshake firm, his eyes bright with satisfaction. Sam clasped his hand, his chuckle warm and genuine, a nod to the alliance sealed by the day's vows.

Laetitia stepped forward, her smile radiant as she pulled Sam into a big hug, her arms wrapping around him with a warmth that spoke of family and ambition fulfilled. "Welcome, Sam," she said, before she stepped back.

Sam nodded, his smile unwavering, as he turned to Eliza. "We should prepare for the journey to Locust Grove," he said. "Mr. Martin is expecting us, and we have a long ride ahead to Nashville."

Eliza nodded silently, her eyes drifting toward the musicians as they packed up their instruments near the yard's edge. Elmore, his back turned, adjusted the straps on his fiddle case, his lean frame taut with a quiet sorrow that pierced her heart. She couldn't help but watch.

Offering his hand, Sam helped his new bride into the carriage, his touch steady but unaware of the storm within her. "Let's make good time," he said to the driver. "We need to arrive before dark."

"Yes, Governor," the driver replied, snapping the reins, the horses trotting briskly as the wagon creaked forward.

Friends and well-wishers gathered to wave, their cheers and smiles a blur to Eliza as she turned to look back, her hands gripping the carriage's edge. Elmore watched the carriage disappear down the road. His shoulders sagged slightly as he turned and walked away.

Eliza leaned out of the wagon, her gaze clinging to him until he vanished from sight. She pressed her hand to her chest, swallowing the lump in her throat, her tears held back by sheer will.

Sam noticed her expression, mistaking her emotion for nerves, and reached for her hand, his grip warm but distant. "We'll spend a day or two at Locust Grove," he said, "and then we'll head on to Nashville. I've received assurances that we'll have the finest room at the Nashville Inn with the grandest view of the river."

Eliza forced a smile, nodding faintly, her voice silent as her mind lingered on the man she'd left behind.

The wagon rolled onward, Allendale shrinking behind them, its white fences and sprawling fields fading into the golden haze of late afternoon. The road stretched ahead, a ribbon of dust winding through rolling hills, the clop of hooves a steady rhythm against the quiet. Sam settled back in his seat, adjusting his hat, his posture relaxed, his eyes on the horizon, a man certain of his path.

Eliza sat stiffly beside him, her shawl slipping slightly, her hands clasped in her lap, the gold ring on her finger a quiet weight. She stared aimlessly at the leafless trees, but her thoughts were elsewhere.

Present Day

The memory slowly drifted away.

Eliza's hands, so frail now, twisted weakly in the worn blanket that covered her. For a moment, she said nothing, her breath rasping softly in the stillness.

Susie sat frozen, her eyes wide with disbelief.

"Mama," she whispered, her voice thick, "why did you go through with it?"

Eliza turned her head slightly on the pillow, her eyes glittering in the low light — not with fever, but with memory.

"Because love," she said hoarsely, "doesn't always win. Not in the world I lived in."

Susie's throat tightened. She reached for Eliza's hand and squeezed it gently.

"I would have run," Susie said, fierce and aching.

Eliza smiled faintly — not bitter, not regretful, but infinitely tired.

"So would I, if I had been you," she murmured. "But I didn't. I was a girl raised to believe a family's name mattered more than a girl's happiness. I believed it until the moment it was too late."

For a long moment, they sat there in silence. Then, Eliza closed her eyes, gathering her strength, and the past pulled her under again.

Locust Grove

January 22, 1829, Nashville, Tennessee

The wagon rolled to a stop before the sprawling Locust Grove mansion, its grand manor framed by towering oaks, their bare branches catching the first delicate flakes of snow that had just begun to fall. The manicured lawn stretched wide under the fading sun, the plantation house's white columns gleaming with quiet elegance, the newborn flurry dusting the ground.

Thomas Martin, in his fifties, strode onto the wide columned porch, his robust frame clad in a tailored coat, his welcoming smile radiating old Southern charm. Beside him bounced Martha, his ten-year-old daughter, bundled in a thick shawl, her cheeks pink from the cold, her lively eyes sparkling with curiosity. "Sam! Welcome back to Locust Grove!" Thomas called, his voice hearty, his arms open as he descended the steps.

Sam Houston hopped down from the wagon, a broad grin splitting his face. "Thomas, it's good to see you," he said, his tone warm with camaraderie. "It's been far too long."

The two men clasped hands warmly. "Far too long indeed," Thomas said, his eyes crinkling with affection. He turned to the wagon, his smile widening. "And this must be your lovely bride."

Sam turned to help Eliza down, his hand steady as she stepped carefully, her gloved hand resting lightly in his, her white lace wedding dress now covered by a thin shawl that did little to ease the chill she barely felt. Her face was calm, but her hazel eyes took in the mansion's grandeur with quiet trepidation. "Thomas, may I present my wife, Eliza," Sam said, his voice proud, his arm guiding her forward.

Thomas smiled warmly, shaking her hand with gentle respect. "Welcome to Locust Grove, Mrs. Houston," he said, his tone rich with hospitality.

Eliza shuddered at the sound of her new last name, though she still managed a polite nod. "Thank you," she said softly.

Martha stepped forward, her shawl slipping slightly as she peered up at Eliza, her curiosity unguarded. "You're very pretty, ma'am," she said, her voice bright, her smile infectious.

Managing a soft smile, Eliza's expression warmed briefly. "Thank you," she said.

Thomas chuckled, ruffling his daughter's hair with an affectionate hand. "Martha's been excited to meet the governor's wife," he said. "Come, let's get you inside before we all freeze." He gestured toward the house as he and Martha led the way.

Sam softly took Eliza's arm as they ascended the steps.

The interior of the mansion was as grand as its exterior, a sweeping staircase dominating the foyer, its polished wood floors gleaming under the warm glow of an ornate chandelier. A roaring fire crackled in the parlor, while the faint scent of baked bread wafted through the air.

Thomas proudly showed off his home, his pride evident in every gesture. "Come on in, let's get you settled," he said, his steps echoing on the hardwood. "I've prepared the east bedroom — the best view of the grounds, if I may say so." He winked at Eliza, his charm effortless, though her nod was polite, her eyes still taking in the unfamiliar splendor around her.

Sam's smile was broad, his voice warm with appreciation. "You've outdone yourself, as always," he said, his hand resting lightly on Eliza's arm.

Martha skipped ahead, her shawl trailing as she peeked into the parlor, her energy uncontainable. "I'll show them, Papa!" she called, bouncing up the stairs.

"Easy now!" Thomas chuckled as he motioned for Sam and Eliza to follow, his stride steady as he ascended the staircase.

Thomas Martin opened the door to a room that seemed as though it had been waiting for them. A fire crackled in the hearth, the rich wood paneling aglow beneath the gentle sway of flames. A grand four-poster bed, its frame adorned with carvings and draped in the finest linens, commanded the center of the room.

"Here we are," Thomas said warmly, stepping back to let them in. "I hope it suits you."

Sam surveyed the room, clearly impressed. "It's perfect, Thomas. Thank you."

Eliza wandered to the tall windows, drawn toward the landscape beyond. Snow drifted steadily down, blanketing the fields in shimmering white.

Thomas paused at the door. "I'll leave you two to settle in," he said. "If there's anything you need, just say the word."

With a quiet nod, he pulled the door shut behind him.

Sam set their bags down, shrugging off his overcoat. For a moment he simply watched her—his new wife, her silhouette framed by firelight and snowfall.

"It's beautiful, isn't it?" he said gently.

Eliza nodded without turning from the window. "Yes... it is," her voice distant.

Sam crossed the room. His tone softened as he drew closer, the bravado of earlier giving way to something more tender, almost pleading.

"Eliza... I know this is all new. But you'll see. I'll take care of you."

Eliza finally turned from the window, her face calm but guarded. Sam stepped closer, his eyes searching hers, trying to decipher the emotions fluttering beneath the surface.

Sam stepped closer as he brushed a stray curl from her neck. She stiffened slightly but she did not move away. "You're my wife now," he whispered. "You're safe with me."

He took her hand in his and guided her gently toward the bed. Eliza's heart pounded as she walked. She sat at the edge, fingers knotting into the bedspread.

Sam removed his coat and began to unfasten the buttons of his waistcoat. He then slipped off his trousers, leaving his shirt untucked against his lean frame. As he moved, Eliza's gaze, seemingly against her will, was drawn to his upper thigh. The fabric of his shirt had caught slightly, revealing a patch of skin marred by an old wound. It looked painful still, as if it had never truly healed.

Eliza gasped, her hand flying to her mouth. "Oh my..." she whispered.

Startled by her reaction, Sam followed her eyes, glancing down at the offending wound. A fleeting shadow of self-consciousness danced across his face, a momentary vulnerability that he quickly masked with a forced nonchalance.

"It's nothing to worry about, dear," he said lightly. "Just an old war wound. I caught an arrow down in Alabama. Never healed the way it should've."

But Eliza wasn't listening. She couldn't tear her eyes away from the scar.

Misreading her silence, Sam stepped closer, trying to reassure her.

"It doesn't trouble me anymore. Truly."

He reached out to touch her shoulder, a gesture meant to comfort, but she recoiled slightly, a subtle flinch that was enough to freeze his hand mid-motion.

Eliza shook her head, voice trembling. "Sam, I... I can't."

Confusion swept across his face, quickly turning into frustration.

"Eliza, it's our wedding night. You're my wife."

She swallowed, tears burning the corners of her eyes.

"I cannot, Sam. I will not."

The confusion in Sam's eyes hardened into anger. He straightened abruptly, pulling his trousers back up in jerky, frustrated movements. His jaw tightened, the muscles clenching as he fastened the buttons with sharp, decisive clicks. His expression darkened, the warmth he had shown earlier completely extinguished.

"You're my wife, Eliza," he stated, his voice firm, bordering on harsh. "This is what's expected of you. Of us."

Eliza's eyes welled with tears that now spilled over, tracing wet paths down her pale cheeks, but she offered no response, no explanation.

Sam glared at her for a long, tense moment, his frustration barely contained. Then, with a sudden, sharp movement, he turned and strode towards the door.

"Suit yourself," he muttered coldly, before slamming the door behind him.

Eliza remained motionless on the edge of the bed, her tears now falling freely, unchecked. Her breath hitched in ragged sobs as she pressed her hands to her face, the muffled sounds lost in the crackling of the fire. The elegant room, meant to be a haven for the newlyweds was now filled with the quiet weeping of a reluctant bride alone on her wedding night.

Present Day

The room was dim, lit only by the soft orange glow of the fire, its light tracing weary lines across Eliza's pale, frail face as she reclined against a stack of pillows. Her eyes were distant, lost in memories too heavy to bear. Susie sat on the edge of the bed, her vibrant energy subdued, replaced by a quiet intensity as she studied her mother's troubled expression.

"Mother, you don't have to tell me more if it's too painful," Susie said softly.

Eliza turned her head slowly, her eyes meeting Susie's, her voice trembling as she spoke, each word a step into a past she'd long buried. "No, Susie," she said, "You deserve to know the truth."

Susie leaned forward, gently clasping her mother's hand, her eyes searching for the story's next piece. "Was he cruel to you?" she asked, her voice barely above a whisper, a flicker of fear in her gaze.

Eliza's face tightened as she took a deep, shuddering breath. "Sam… Sam was not an easy man," she said, her voice breaking, her eyes turning to the fire, its glow reflecting the pain she carried. "He was used to being obeyed, respected. And I… I couldn't give him what he wanted."

Her voice cracked slightly as she continued, each word a confession. "I… I thought I was doing what was right," she said, her tone tinged with regret. "Marrying him was supposed to secure my future, my family's future. But from the moment I said, 'I do,' I felt as though I'd lost myself."

Susie tilted her head, her eyes softening as she watched her mother wrestle with the past. "Sam started as a man of grand gestures," she said, a faint bitterness threading her words. "Lavish promises, powerful words… He made me feel like I could be part of something greater than myself."

Her tone hardened slightly, her head shaking as if to dispel the illusion. "But when I pulled away from him, when I didn't give him the devotion he demanded, he… changed," she said, her voice dropping to a near whisper.

Susie stiffened, her breath catching, her voice sharp with concern. "Changed how?" she asked, her eyes wide, searching her mother's face for answers.

Eliza exhaled sharply. "He grew colder," she said, her gaze distant. "Meaner. I became something to conquer rather than cherish."

She paused, the fire's soft pops a counterpoint to the pain in her words. "I realized, too late, that I had made a mistake," she said, with a noticeable glimmer in her eyes. "But by then, I was his wife."

The room fell silent. Susie's hand tightened around her mother's.

January 22, 1829, Nashville, Tennessee

Downstairs, in the parlor, Thomas Martin sat in a high-backed chair, a crystal tumbler in hand. The amber liquid reflected the firelight as he savored a quiet moment after a busy day preparing for his guests.

The door creaked open, and Sam Houston stepped inside, his tailored suit rumpled from travel, his tie loosened at the collar. His face carried a shadow of frustration. Thomas looked up, his smile faltering with surprise, his brow lifting as he set his glass on the side table. "Sam? I thought you retired back to your room for the evening," he said, his voice warm but curious.

Sam mumbled, his hand brushing through his hair as he crossed to the fireplace. "We rode all the way from Gallatin in that damned carriage in the cold," he said. "Eliza doesn't feel well."

Thomas raised a skeptical eyebrow. "Long day for a bride," he replied. He gestured to the decanter on the table. "Care for a drink?"

Sam nodded. "I would," he said, as he sank into a chair opposite Thomas.

Thomas poured a generous amount of whiskey into a fresh tumbler, handing it to Sam with a knowing smile. Sam took it, downing the first glass in a single swallow, the burn a fleeting distraction from his frustration upstairs. Without another word, Thomas refilled it, and then again, the clink of crystal a quiet rhythm as Sam drank one after another, his shoulders slumping with each glass, his silence growing heavier.

Thomas sipped his drink, his eyes studying his friend, but he asked no more, letting the silence speak for itself.

♦ ♦ ♦ ♦ ♦ ♦

In the east bedroom, Eliza sat on the edge of the bed, still clad in her wedding dress. Her eyes were red and puffy from earlier tears, her face pale, her gaze fixed on the fireplace.

The door creaked open, and Sam Houston stumbled inside, a half-empty glass of whiskey in hand, the sharp scent of alcohol clinging to him. His coat was slung over one arm, his tie loosened and askew, his boots scuffing against the floor as he shut the door with a sharp snap, the sound jarring in the quiet room. His face was cold, bitter, his eyes narrowed as they landed on Eliza, a storm of hurt and anger brewing beneath his drunken haze.

"You're still awake," he said, his voice slurred, his gaze piercing.

Eliza didn't respond, her eyes fixed on the fireplace, her body rigid, as if silence could shield her from him. Sam snorted, his voice cutting through the stillness, harsh and biting. "Maybe I shouldn't be surprised," he said. "I imagine you don't sleep well, being as cold as you are."

Eliza tensed, but she didn't turn to look at him. Sam's words grew sharper, his anger fueled by whiskey and wounded pride. "You know, it's remarkable," he said, his voice venomous. "Riding in that cold carriage, wind biting at my face, I felt warmer than I do standing next to you."

His words struck like a blade, each one laced with hurt and rage, the whiskey amplifying his scorn. "A man goes to war, survives wounds that would kill lesser men, fights his way to the governor's chair, and what does he get?" he said, his voice rising, his glass trembling in his hand. "A wife who won't even touch him on their wedding night."

Eliza's voice trembled as she finally spoke, her words soft but raw, a plea born of exhaustion. "Sam, please…" she said, her eyes still on the embers.

He cut her off, his voice booming, his face flushed with anger. "Please? Please what, Eliza?" he snapped, his words a lash. "Please pretend that I didn't make the biggest mistake of my life marrying you?"

His words struck deep, Eliza flinched. She blinked back tears, refusing to let them fall in front of him.

Sam downed the rest of his whiskey, slamming the glass onto the dresser with a force that echoed through the room.

"You're not just cold—you are an empty, ungrateful little girl who doesn't understand the first thing about what it means to stand beside a man of my stature," he said, his voice dripping with disdain, his eyes boring into her.

Eliza's hands trembled, her breath shallow, but she remained silent. Sam stared at her for a moment. Then, with a disgusted shake of his head, he muttered under his breath, "God help me."

He shrugged off his coat, tossing it carelessly onto a chair, his movements sloppy as he kicked off his boots. He made his way to the bed, crawling in with rough, clumsy motions, pulling the covers over himself with a jerk, his back to Eliza.

"Goodnight, Miss Eliza," he snarled, his voice thick with contempt.

Within moments, the sound of his thunderous, drunken snores filled the room, a harsh rhythm that grated against the quiet. Eliza sat frozen on the edge of the bed, her eyes locked on the glass he'd left on the dresser.

After a moment, she slowly rose to her feet as she crossed to the nightstand. She blew out the oil lamp, plunging the room into darkness, save for the faint glow of the dying fire. Eliza climbed into the bed, her movements careful to avoid disturbing Sam, curling up on the edge of the mattress, as far from him as possible.

Silent tears slipped down her cheeks as she buried her face in the pillow, her shoulders trembling with quiet sobs, each one a release of the pain she could no longer contain.

January 23, 1829, Gallatin, Tennessee

The morning light poured through the curtains of the east bedroom, the room bright with the radiant glow of snow blanketing the ground outside. The fireplace's embers smoldered faintly, their warmth long faded, but the snow's light filled the space with a deceptive clarity, illuminating the bed where Eliza stirred beneath the covers. Her face was pale and drawn, her eyes puffy from the tears that had soaked her pillow, the weight of Sam's venomous words settling over her like a bruise.

Muffled laughter seeped through the window, punctuated by the occasional shriek of delight, a joyous commotion that pierced the room's thick silence. Eliza sat up slowly. She tilted her head, listening, her brow furrowing as the sounds of play tugged at her curiosity, a fleeting distraction from the night before.

Wrapping a shawl around her shoulders, she pulled herself out of bed. Still in her wedding dress, she crossed to the window and drew the curtain aside. As the bright light spilled across her face, she found the grounds had been transformed into a canvas of white. Sam Houston stood at the center of a group of laughing children, their coats and scarves bright against the snow. Some were building snowmen, while others pelted each other with snowballs. Crouched behind a low stone wall, Sam pretended to duck for cover, his hearty laughter ringing out as snowballs thudded against his makeshift fort. His cheeks were flushed from the cold and exertion, his black coat dusted with snow, his smile broad and infectious, a governor at play.

Eliza watched in silence. The Sam Houston before her was the man Tennessee adored—charming, larger than life, a hero who could win hearts with a laugh. But his words from the night before— "empty, ungrateful little girl"—cut through the laughter, a blade that left her raw. She stepped away from the window, pulled on her coat and slipped on her gloves.

The yard crackled underfoot as Eliza stepped into the snow, her boots sinking into it with every step.

Children darted across the yard, their scarves trailing behind them as they chased one another, laughter ringing through the air. Sam was at the center of it all— his coat dusted white, his booming laughter rising above the rest as he ducked behind a snowman, narrowly missing a well-aimed snowball.

From the edge of the gathering, Martha stood bundled in a dark wool coat, her cheeks pink, her breath forming small clouds as she smiled warmly at the playful chaos.

She spotted Eliza and waved her over. "It seems the Governor is getting the worst of the snowballing," Martha said with a chuckle. "You had better go out and help him."

Eliza glanced toward Sam just as he looked up and spotted her.

In an instant, the easy grin vanished from his face. A dark scowl bore into her soul—a flash of resentment so sharp it felt like a slap across the frozen air.

The blow struck deeper than it should have.

Eliza's fingers tightened around her shawl as a hot flush of anger boiled up inside her, cutting through the cold like a blade.

"I wish they would kill him," she said under her breath.

Martha's smile faltered.

"What?" she asked, laughing uncertainly, as if she had misheard.

Eliza didn't blink.

Her voice came again, flat, without emotion. "I wish from the bottom of my heart that they would kill him."

Martha stared, her mouth parting in disbelief. "Eliza… you can't mean that."

But Eliza said nothing. She turned and strode away, the snow crunching loudly beneath her boots.

The children's laughter faded behind her, swallowed by the brittle, empty cold.

An hour later, in the dining room, Eliza sat across from Thomas nibbling on some biscuits and ham. Thomas, mid-story, gestured animatedly with his fork, his eyes twinkling as he spoke. "And when that mule finally stopped," he said, shaking his head, "I swear, the poor fool holding the reins was as white as the snow outside!"

Eliza chuckled—her first real smile in days. "I can't imagine you keeping a straight face through that," she said, a playful gleam twinkling in her eyes.

Thomas chuckled, reaching for his coffee. "Oh, I didn't. I laughed so hard I scared the horses."

Their laughter tangled together, warm and effortless.

But the moment broke with the low creak of the door.

Sam stepped inside, brushing snow from his coat. His cheeks were flushed from the cold, his boots leaving wet tracks across the floor. Without a word, he crossed to the fire, rubbing his hands briskly before the flames.

Eliza's smile disappeared. She dropped her eyes to her plate, the coffee in her cup suddenly more interesting than anything else in the room.

Thomas, ever the gracious host, broke the silence with a wide smile. "Ah, Sam! Out for a morning stroll in this weather?"
Sam turned, offering a nod, his voice warm enough but carrying an edge underneath.

"I was until I was ambushed by the children. The snow's still falling, but it's not as bad as last night."

His eyes flickered toward Eliza—just a glance—but the look hardened something in his face before he turned back to Thomas, letting the moment pass unspoken.

"We'll need to depart tomorrow," he added. "The roads should be passable by then, and I have business waiting for me in town."

Thomas set down his fork, glancing sideways at Sam, sensing the shift in the room. "So soon? Surely you can stay a few more days."

Sam shook his head, his tone firm but polite. "I appreciate your hospitality, Thomas. Truly. But the people of Tennessee won't wait for the weather to clear."

Thomas hesitated, his eyes moving between Sam and Eliza, who stirred her coffee absently, her focus far away.

"Well, the offer stands," Thomas said finally, his voice a little quieter. "You're always welcome here."

Sam managed a faint grin.
"Thank you."

For a long moment, nothing moved but the flames in the hearth.

Then, Eliza rose, her chair scraping softly against the floor. She gathered her coffee in one hand, the other tugging her shawl tighter around her shoulders.

"Excuse me," she said, her voice almost a whisper, steady, and utterly detached.

Without another glance at either man, she walked from the room, her footsteps almost soundless against the wooden floor.

Thomas watched her go, wondering what was wrong. He waited a beat, then turned back to Sam. "Is everything all right?" he asked carefully.

Sam didn't answer right away. He stared into the fire for moment before he finally spoke. "Marriage is an adjustment," he said finally, the words clipped and hard. "She'll be fine."

Thomas nodded slowly, though his face showed he wasn't convinced. He knew enough to leave the matter alone.

♦ ♦ ♦ ♦ ♦ ♦

The snow had finally stopped by afternoon, leaving the world outside bathed in a clean, blinding white. The landscape stretched wide and empty beyond the frosted windows, beautiful and cold all at once.

Eliza sat curled into a chair by the window, a Bible open on her lap. The fire crackled quietly across the room. She turned a page, her fingers moving automatically, but her eyes didn't follow the words.

Her gaze shifted to the window instead, drawn again and again to the endless sweep of snow — the way it smothered everything in sight, silencing it all under a perfect, suffocating hush.

From somewhere down the hall, she heard the deep rumble of Sam's voice, followed by Thomas' easy laughter. The low clink of glasses carried through the house.

She pressed the edge of the Bible tighter against her lap, willing herself to focus, to stay present. But the words blurred on the page.

Another gust of laughter echoed from the other room—louder this time, freer, as if the weight that pressed on her chest didn't exist in theirs.

She turned her face to the cold glass, letting it bite her skin, welcoming the numbness.

♦ ♦ ♦ ♦ ♦ ♦

That night, Sam stumbled into the bedroom, trailing the sharp scent of whiskey.

Without a glance her way, he fell into bed, his snores filling the space between them like a living thing.

Eliza lay rigid, her hands fisted in the blankets.

The dying fire cast faint shadows on the ceiling, each movement whispering of a future already slipping beyond her reach.

A single tear escaped, tracing her cheek as the darkness swallowed the last of the light. Beside her, Sam snored on, oblivious.

Eliza closed her eyes, surrendering herself to a restless, broken sleep.

The Nashville Inn

January 24, 1829, Nashville, Tennessee

The carriage rumbled to a halt outside a large inn overlooking the frozen Cumberland River. Dusk had settled over Nashville, the last light fading behind a veil of mist and low clouds. Warm golden lanterns glowed behind the inn's windows, promising shelter from the cold.

A stable hand hurried forward, his boots crunching in the snow. Sam stepped down first and then turned to help Eliza, his hand steady as she descended the carriage steps, her fingers light on his.

"Come now," Sam said, his voice brisk but not unkind. "Let's get inside."

Eliza nodded, her cheeks pale from the cold, her breath forming small clouds in the air.

Inside, the inn welcomed them with a rush of heat and the comforting roar of a fire blazing in the hearth. Sam shrugged out of his coat, already scanning the room with a soldier's instinct, while Eliza stood still for a moment, letting the warmth seep into her frozen limbs.

As they moved further into the lobby, several well-dressed individuals came forward to greet Sam, their voices a mix of admiration and enthusiasm.

"We read about your marriage in the paper, Governor!" one man exclaimed, a broad grin on his face. "It's an honor to meet you and your lovely new wife!"

Another woman, her eyes wide with excitement, chimed in, "How fortunate we are to have you both here tonight!"

Sam gave a tight-lipped smile, acknowledging the well-wishers with a polite nod. But his attention quickly turned toward Judge John Overton, who had approached with a strong, respectable presence.

"Sam!" Overton boomed, his voice warm and booming, yet tempered with respect. "It's been too long, my friend."

Sam's face softened as he shook the judge's hand firmly. "John, it's always a pleasure," he said, his voice steady, yet with a hint of weariness.

As the group continued to murmur in the background, Sam turned to Eliza, his arm gently guiding her closer. "This is my new bride, Eliza," he said, his tone a touch proud but with a slight edge of impatience.

Eliza offered a small, friendly smile, her eyes scanning the room with a guarded detachment. "It's a pleasure to meet you all," she said quietly, her voice soft but betraying the unease that settled in her chest.

Sam, picking up on her discomfort, glanced back toward the crowd. "I'll get my bride settled in and then join you all downstairs," he said, his tone carrying a note of finality, as if eager to escape the well-wishers and the bustling chatter.

Eliza gave a subtle sigh of relief as Sam led her up the stairs, leaving the crowd behind as they disappeared into the warmth of their room.

♦ ♦ ♦ ♦ ♦ ♦

Their room upstairs was smaller than Eliza expected; but it was still cozy. A large four-poster bed stood beneath the low rafters, a fire crackling in the fireplace, and a single window framed a view of the frozen river.

Eliza removed her cloak, standing close to the fire, her hands stretched toward the flames. Sam set their bags down and glanced around, nodding with approval.

"It's a fine room," he said after a moment, his voice softer. "Nice view of the river."

Eliza nodded faintly, offering a tight, polite smile. "Yes... it's very nice."

For a beat, Sam lingered, watching her. The tension between them hummed.

He cleared his throat awkwardly.

"You look... lovely, Eliza."

She turned, caught off guard by the compliment. A ghost of a smile flashed across her face, but the distance between them was still there, wide and aching.

"Thank you," she said quietly.

Sam shifted, fidgeting with the edge of his coat. "I saw Judge Overton downstairs when we arrived. Thought I'd go have a word with him."

Eliza glanced back at the fire, her voice barely above a whisper. "Of course."

He hesitated, as if wanting to say more but finding no words. Finally, he adjusted his coat and moved toward the door.

"I won't be too long," he said, pausing at the threshold.

He turned, offering one last look over his shoulder. "Really, Eliza... you look beautiful tonight."

She didn't answer. She just watched him go, the door clicking softly shut behind him.

The room was silent except for the occasional pop of the fire. Eliza stood still for a long moment, then her gaze moved to the small desk tucked beside the window.

A single sheet of paper, an inkwell, and a pen rested there, almost as if waiting for her.

Slowly, she crossed the room and sat down. Her hand hovered over the paper, hesitating, before she dipped the pen and began to write. The words poured from her like water breaching a dam—aching, desperate, unspoken truths spilling out faster than she could stop them.

Footsteps sounded faintly in the corridor. She paused, heart pounding, but when they faded, she returned to the letter.

She was nearly finished when the door flew open with a bang, startling her. The pen slipped from her fingers, leaving a dark blot on the page.

Sam strode into the room, a glass of whiskey clutched in one hand.

"The judge has already left," he muttered, setting the glass down on a side table.

He tilted his head as his eyes dropped to the desk—and to Eliza's hands, where she clutched the hastily folded letter.

His eyes narrowed.

"What is this?"

Eliza snatched the letter to her chest, her voice catching.

"Nothing," she stammered. "I was just—"

But Sam was already crossing the room in a few swift strides. He ripped the letter from her trembling hands.

"Sam, please! Don't!" she cried.

He ignored her, unfolding the letter, his eyes scanning the page. His expression darkened instantly.

"Elmore," he said flatly, his voice cutting through

the room like a blade.

His gaze snapped to Eliza, burning with fury, before he turned back to the letter, his voice growing louder with every line he read.

"Since the day I saw you at the wedding, I haven't stopped thinking of you... You've been on my mind every second... I've made a terrible mistake..."

His hand trembled slightly as he lowered the page, his jaw tightening hard enough to whiten his knuckles.

With a sharp, deliberate movement, he tore the letter in half. Then again. And again. Letting the pieces fall to the floor.

He turned on her, his voice rising.

"You've been thinking of him? Every second since our wedding?"

Eliza said nothing. Tears welled in her eyes.

"You ungrateful, foolish girl," Sam snapped. "Do you have any idea what you're risking? What people will say? What the General will think?"

He took a step toward her, looming, the rage radiating from him like heat.

"You're my wife, Eliza. Mine."

In a sudden, terrible moment, he raised his hand as if to strike her.

Eliza recoiled, her breath catching in a terrified gasp.

Sam froze. His hand trembled in the air, hovering there like an accusation. His face twisted with a mix of rage, grief, and something deeper—something like shame.

After a long, shuddering moment, he dropped his hand.

His voice, when it came, was low and venomous.

"You're not worth it."

He turned around, yanking the door open so violently it rattled on its hinges.

"Foul, evil siren," he muttered, almost under his breath, before slamming the door behind him with a crash that shook the walls.

The silence that followed was deafening.

Eliza sank onto the edge of the bed, her body trembling from the inside out. Tears streamed silently down her face, her hands limp in her lap, her chest heaving with the quiet, broken rhythm of grief.

At her feet, the torn scraps of her letter lay scattered like fallen leaves after a storm — words she could never take back.

She stared at them for a long time, her vision blurred with tears. Slowly, as if her body moved without permission, she reached down and picked up one little piece. Her fingers trembled around it.

She let it fall.

It fluttered to the floor.

With a shuddering breath, Eliza crawled under the quilt, pulling it up to her chin as if it could protect her from the cold that had nothing to do with the winter outside. She curled into a tight ball, her knees tucked against her chest.

Her tears soaked into the pillow, muffling her soft, broken sobs.

The fire dwindled.

The cold crept closer.

And somewhere between grief and exhaustion, Eliza fell into a restless, haunted sleep.

Alone.

January 25, 1829, Nashville, Tennessee

The faint light of dawn crept into the room, slipping through the thin curtains and washing the floor in pale, tired gray. The fire in the hearth had burned down to little more than ashes and the occasional soft crackle of dying embers.

The door creaked open.

Sam stumbled inside, the scent of whiskey trailing behind him like a shadow. His boots scuffed against the floorboards as he paused just inside the room, blinking against the dim light.

His gaze moved instinctively toward the bed.

Empty.

The covers lay flat and cold.

Sam scowled, his eyes sweeping the room more carefully now. He caught sight of the wardrobe—half open. The bag that had rested at the foot of the bed was gone. So was her shawl.

He froze and exhaled sharply. Confusion clouded his face first—then frustration, then something else, something painful he couldn't quite bury.

He staggered forward, his boots dragging, and dropped heavily onto the edge of the bed, his elbows braced against his knees. His hands rose to cover his face, fingers tangling in his hair.

The world swayed around him.

When he lifted his head, his eyes fell to the desk.

Among the torn pieces of the letter lay a single gold wedding band, small and unassuming, shining weakly in the gray light.

For a long time, he just sat there, hollow and still, as the morning crept slowly over the frozen river outside.

Return to Allendale

January 25, 1829, Gallatin, Tennessee

The late afternoon sun hung low over Allendale. The world had shifted since Eliza left. The snow clung stubbornly in scattered patches, but most had melted into slush, leaving the yard soft and muddied.

From the porch, John Allen stepped out into the crisp air, pulling his coat tighter around himself. His breath rose in faint puffs as he adjusted his scarf and gazed down the long, winding drive. The landscape was quiet except for the soft, steady crunch of melting snow underfoot.

At first, he thought he was imagining the figure that appeared at the far end of the lane—small, burdened, moving unevenly up the muddy path.

But as the figure came closer, the truth became undeniable.

It was Eliza.

She struggled under the weight of a large bag, her boots squelching in the mud, the hem of her cloak dark with wetness and torn from the road. Her cheeks were flushed with cold, but it was the raw, broken look in her eyes that made John's heart seize.

He took a step forward, confusion flashing across his face before recognition struck him like a blow.

"Eliza?" he called, his voice rough with disbelief.

At the sound of her father's voice, Eliza lifted her head. Tears streaked her reddened cheeks, her lip trembling as she tried to quicken her pace, stumbling over a hidden patch of snow.

John didn't hesitate. He bounded down the steps, boots splashing through slush and mud.

By the time he reached her, Eliza dropped the bag with a thud and collapsed against him, her small body wracked with sobs.

"I couldn't..." she gasped, clutching at the fabric of his coat as if it were the only thing holding her up. "I couldn't stay."

John wrapped his arms around her tightly, pressing his hand to the back of her head. His face was a mixture of worry and fierce protectiveness.

"You're home now," he murmured against her hair, voice thick with emotion. "That's all that matters."

For a long moment, he simply held her as she wept.

Finally, glancing up at the big, silent house behind him, he gathered her bag in one hand and tucked her trembling body under his arm.

"Come inside and get warm," he said gently.

Together, they climbed the steps onto the porch.

As they crossed the threshold, John pulled the door closed behind them with a soft click, shutting out the dying winter light—and the world Eliza had left behind.

◆ ◆ ◆ ◆ ◆ ◆

The parlor was quiet except for the soft clink of a teaspoon against porcelain. Eliza sat curled at one end of the couch, a cup of tea cradled in her trembling hands. The fire crackled faintly in the hearth.

Her mother, Laetitia, hovered close by, her face etched with worry despite the careful composure she tried to maintain. Across the room, John Allen paced in heavy, deliberate steps, his expression dark and brooding.

Laetitia lowered herself onto the couch beside Eliza, smoothing her skirts with a trembling hand.

"Eliza," she said gently, "what happened?" Eliza stared into her tea, her eyes fixed on the rippling surface. The silence stretched between them, thick and suffocating.

John stopped pacing, his voice sharp with barely restrained anger.

"Did he hurt you?"

Eliza flinched slightly at the force of his words, but she shook her head.

"No... He didn't lay a hand on me."

Laetitia reached out, placing a comforting hand on her daughter's knee. Her touch was light but steady. "Whatever it is, we'll fix it," she said softly. "You're home now."

Eliza nodded faintly, her fingers tightening around the teacup as fresh tears slipped down her cheeks. She lifted her eyes to her father, her voice trembling.

"I'm sorry."

John's stern expression cracked. He stepped closer and placed a reassuring hand on her shoulder.

"There's nothing to be sorry for," he said tenderly.

Eliza nodded again, a small, broken motion, as if she were trying to convince herself.

"I don't know what to do," she whispered, her voice cracking wide open.

Laetitia wasted no time. She set the teacup aside and pulled Eliza into her arms, holding her tightly against her shoulder.

"We'll figure it out, Eliza," she murmured into her

hair. "Together."

Eliza leaned into her mother's embrace.

The fire crackled on, the room closing around them in a fragile, aching kind of peace—the first steps toward healing, but not without scars.

♦ ♦ ♦ ♦ ♦ ♦

Later that evening, Eliza stood by the dresser as she unpacked her things.

When the last piece was folded away, she moved to the vanity and sat down. Her reflection stared back at her, pale and hollow-eyed, a ghost of the girl who had left home not so long ago. The bruised redness around her eyes betrayed the tears she had fought—and lost—all day.

Eliza tilted her head slightly, studying herself as if searching for something she couldn't name, something she was no longer certain even existed.

She picked up a brush and ran it slowly through her hair.

Eliza straightened her posture, her fingers pausing mid-stroke.

In her reflection, the faintest spark glinted in her eyes—something raw and fragile, but alive. Determination. The kind that didn't come from strength, but from surviving the moment you thought would break you.

The brush dropped to the vanity with a soft clatter. Eliza stared at herself a moment longer, then inhaled deeply, drawing the breath all the way down to the hollow ache inside her.

Present Day

Eliza shifted weakly against her pillows.

Susie sat on the bed, her eyes never leaving her mother's face.

Eliza's voice, though soft, carried the weight of years.

"I remember coming home," she said, her gaze drifting toward the window as if she could still see the dusty road that had carried her back. "It wasn't the same place I left. Or maybe I wasn't the same girl."

She paused, gathering her breath.

"The house felt smaller somehow. Quiet.

Susie said nothing, but her throat bobbed as she swallowed hard.

"I couldn't bring myself to look my momma or daddy in the eye. Funny thing is, they didn't say much either."

She leaned her head back against the pillows, struggling to get comfortable.

"I spent my days up in that old room," she continued, her voice growing stronger for a moment. "Starin' at the same doll on the shelf, the same mirror on the vanity. I thought if I stayed quiet enough, maybe the walls would forget me. Maybe I'd forget myself."

Eliza exhaled sharply as the fireplace wood crackled softly.

"I cried for a few days," Eliza admitted, her lips curling in a faint, sheepish smile. "Felt sorry for myself." She turned her head slightly, meeting Susie's tear-bright gaze.

Susie reached for her mother's hand, her fingers threading gently through Eliza's fragile ones.

Eliza squeezed back, the smallest ghost of strength still in her grip.

"But then I did what everyone should do when they lose it all — I went to church!"

Amazing Grace

February 13, 1829, Gallatin, Tennessee

The church was bathed in the warm glow of lanterns hanging from the wooden beams.

A small crowd sat scattered across the pews, heads bowed in quiet reflection, soaking in the soothing melody of a fiddle that floated through the room.

At the front, near the pulpit, Elmore stood with his fiddle tucked beneath his chin. His bow glided effortlessly across the strings, the hymn spilling forth with raw, aching emotion. The notes hung in the air, weaving around the congregation.

The sound of the church door creaking open disrupted the stillness.

Heads turned briefly toward the noise but quickly refocused on the music.

Eliza stepped inside, her movements hesitant, almost reluctant. She clutched her shawl tightly around her shoulders, her fingers trembling slightly. Her eyes scanned the room before finding him—Elmore, fully immersed in his playing.

For a moment, he didn't notice. His eyes were closed, lost in an old hymn.

And then, as if drawn by something unseen, he looked up.

Their eyes met across the room.

The connection was instant. Electrifying. Unmistakable.

Elmore's hand slipped, causing his bow to scrape an off-key note that broke the perfect flow of the hymn.

He winced, quickly correcting himself, pouring back into the music as if nothing had happened.

Eliza slipped into the last pew, her movements careful, deliberate. She kept her eyes on Elmore, her heart hammering against her ribs. The lantern light shimmered and cast a golden glow across his face as he played, every note laced with something deeper, something meant for her.

Then, as the opening notes of "*Amazing Grace*" filled the air and the congregation began to sing, a deeper resonance reverberated in Eliza's chest. The melody seemed to speak to her directly, stirring something deep within. It wasn't just the beauty of the song or the tenderness in Elmore's playing — it was the message itself.

She had once been lost, living in a world shaped by the expectations of others, trying to conform to a life that didn't feel like her own. *"I once was lost, but now I'm found,"* the congregation sang. And as Eliza heard the words, they wrapped around her heart. The world had seemed so uncertain, and her choices had been so limited. But now, standing there in that church, she was beginning to see the possibility of something more. *"Was blind, but now I see."*

As the hymn came to its soft, reverent end, Reverend Hume stepped forward from the side of the pulpit.

"Let us pray," he said, his voice steady and familiar.

The congregation bowed their heads, a hush falling over the room. Only the soft rustle of fabric and the occasional clearing of a throat disturbed the quiet. But Eliza remained upright. Her eyes stayed fixed on Elmore.

Across the room, Elmore stood tall beside Hume,

his fiddle lowered but still clutched tightly in his hands. His gaze locked onto Eliza's and did not waver. His expression was a mixture of surprise, longing, and something close to fear—a desperate kind of hope he hadn't dared to name until now.

"Our Father, who art in heaven..." Hume began, his voice droning gently through the room. But the words barely registered for either of them.

For a suspended, breathless moment, the world shrank until it was just the two of them across the expanse of pews and prayers. A fragile line stretched between them, taut and trembling, almost visible in the lantern light.

A soft "Amen" echoed through the church as the prayer ended, and slowly, the congregation lifted their heads.

Eliza flushed, pulling her shawl tighter as she glanced down quickly, her heart pounding. Elmore gripped his fiddle harder, his gaze remaining on her for a long moment before he finally looked away, swallowing hard.

The service continued, Hume's voice rising again as he launched into his sermon, but the magic of that single glance lingered like smoke after a fire.

In that sacred moment, sitting in the back of a quiet church with the weight of her past still clinging to her, Eliza felt something she hadn't felt in months.

Hope.

The congregation slowly began to stir as Reverend Hume closed his Bible, the last echoes of the sermon fading into the rafters. People rose from the pews in small clusters, buttoning coats and pulling shawls tight against the winter chill waiting outside.

Standing near the back, Eliza smoothed the folds of her cloak with trembling fingers. She could feel her heart pounding harder than it should have, her body thrumming with nervous energy.

Near the pulpit, Elmore carefully tucked his fiddle into its case, his eyes flickering toward the back of the church. When he looked up and saw her standing there, a visible breath caught in his chest.

For a moment, neither of them moved.

Gathering what little courage he had, Elmore took a step toward her.

"Eliza," he started, almost hopeful.

But before he could reach her, Reverend Hume's voice rang out over the milling crowd.

"Elmore! A word, if you please."

Elmore hesitated, torn, glancing once toward the pulpit where the reverend stood waving him over.

When he turned back, Eliza was already slipping away.

She caught his eye as she slipped out—a fleeting glance, a shy, almost secret smile curving her lips. Then she disappeared into the shifting crowd.

Elmore stood frozen for a beat, staring after her, the words he hadn't had the chance to say still burning on his tongue.

He sighed, the weight of disappointment burdensome in his chest, and turned reluctantly toward the front of the church.

"Coming, Reverend," he called, his voice rougher than he intended.

As he walked away, he couldn't help but glance one last time toward the door where she had vanished, a part of him wondering if he had imagined it all—the look, the smile, the silent invitation he hadn't been fast enough to answer.

But deep down, he knew it had been real.

♦ ♦ ♦ ♦ ♦ ♦

The night had settled in by the time Eliza reached the gates of Allendale. The sky overhead was a dark velvet, studded with stars, and the damp earth squelched under her boots as she made her way up the path toward the porch.

The house loomed before her, warm light glowing behind the frosted windows, welcoming and foreboding all at once.

When she opened the front door, she wasn't surprised to find her mother waiting.

Arms folded across her chest, Laetitia Allen stood firmly in the foyer, her face composed but tight. The air between them crackled with unspoken words.

Eliza closed the door gently behind her, slipping off her shawl with slow, careful movements.

"Where have you been?" Laetitia asked, her voice sharp in the stillness.

Eliza avoided her mother's eyes as she hung the shawl on the hook by the door.

"I went to church," she said quietly.

Laetitia's gaze sharpened.

"You're still a married woman, Eliza. You need to

respect your husband."

Eliza turned to face her mother fully, her voice trembling with frustration.

"I'm not going back to Nashville," she said, louder than she intended. "I'm not going back to him."

An oppressive silence fell between them.

Laetitia stared at her daughter for a long moment, her expression unreadable. Eliza braced herself for an argument, for disappointment, for judgment.

Instead, Laetitia exhaled sharply, the fight seeming to drain from her all at once.

Without a word, she crossed the room and pulled Eliza into a tight embrace.

Caught off guard, Eliza stiffened at first—then melted into her mother's arms, burying her face against Laetitia's shoulder as fresh tears welled in her eyes.

Laetitia held her tightly, smoothing her hand over Eliza's hair in slow, soothing strokes.

"I just want you to be happy," she whispered.

Eliza nodded against her shoulder, too overwhelmed to speak.

And for the first time in what felt like forever, she believed—if only for a moment—that happiness might still be possible.

The following afternoon at Thomas Boyers' General Store, Thomas carefully stacked ledgers and wrapped up the day's receipts.

Elmore wiped his hands on a rag as he moved toward the front door.

"See you tomorrow, Mr. Boyers," he said, his voice

warm but tired.

Thomas nodded, offering a tired smile. "Good night."

Elmore shrugged into his coat and stepped outside, the cool evening air nipping at his cheeks. The street was quiet, the town settling into the soft hush of twilight.

Elmore tucked his hands into his pockets and started walking.

As he passed the small church, he noticed movement out of the corner of his eye.

Eliza sat on the front steps, her cloak wrapped tightly around her, her hands folded in her lap. She looked small and uncertain.

"Elmore," she called softly.

He froze in place, blinking as if she might disappear if he moved too quickly.

He didn't know what to say.

Neither did she.

They stared at each other for a long moment, the quiet stretching between them, full of things neither of them could quite put into words.

Finally, Eliza rose to her feet and stepped down from the stairs.

"I made a mistake," she said, her voice trembling but clear.

"My life... my life is here. In Gallatin. I'm not going back to Nashville."

Elmore's brows drew together. He searched her expression, looking for some sign he was misunderstanding.

Eliza swallowed hard and pressed on.

"I've thought about you," she whispered. "Every second I've been away."

The words hung in the air between them, delicate and desperate.

Elmore opened his mouth, but nothing came out. Finally, he managed to stammer,

"What about the governor?"

Eliza shook her head slowly, her eyes never leaving his.

"I don't want to be with him," she said, her voice steady now. "I want to be with you."

For a heartbeat, neither of them moved.

Then, without waiting for his answer, Eliza leaned in and pressed her lips to his—a kiss that was soft, tentative, full of every unsaid thing between them.

Elmore pulled away, startled, his heart hammering against his ribs. His mind screamed caution, but his heart... his heart ached in ways he could no longer deny.

He looked into her eyes, searching, questioning, afraid.

She didn't say anything. She only looked at him, her whole soul laid bare in that pleading, desperate gaze.

And then, slowly, as if pulled by something greater than either of them, he leaned back in.

This time, the kiss was different—hungry, passionate, full of months of longing and sorrow and hope twisted together. Elmore pulled her against him, her hands tangling in the fabric of his coat as he kissed her like a drowning man finally finding air.

The world around them—the town, the governor, the expectations—faded into nothing.

For that one stolen moment, there was only them.

"This Belongs to You"

March 2, 1829, Gallatin, Tennessee

Eliza, Ann, and Elmore stepped out of Boyers' General Store, each cradling an apple in their hands. The dark red fruit gleamed in the late winter light.

Ann bit into hers eagerly, laughing as juice trickled down her chin.

"I've never had an apple this sweet!" she exclaimed, wiping her mouth with the back of her hand.

Eliza grinned, raising an eyebrow.
"Or you've just never eaten anything slow enough to taste it."

Ann laughed, unabashed.
"Guilty!"

The three of them laughed together, carefree and loud in the open square, their joy bubbling over like a forgotten melody.

Elmore chuckled as he wiped his fingers on a handkerchief, his smile quieter but just as genuine.

"I think you're both just competing to see who can make the biggest mess," he said, shaking his head.

Eliza flashed a playful smile as she dried her hands.

"And I think you're too polite to admit we've embarrassed you."

"Maybe just a little," he teased.

Their laughter carried across the square, drawing a few curious glances.

People slowed as they passed, some stopping altogether. Conversations hushed. Whispered words floated on the breeze.

Across the way, two well-dressed women stood huddled together, their expressions sharp with judgment.

"Isn't that Mrs. Houston?" one of them whispered, her eyes wide with scandal.

"The governor's wife... with him?" the other answered, shaking her head, her voice dripping with disapproval.

Eliza caught the murmurs, caught the stares—but for the first time in what felt like years, she didn't care.

She laughed louder, her face flushed with happiness, the sunlight catching in her hair. She tossed the last bite of her apple into a nearby barrel, brushing her sticky hands on her skirts without a second thought.

Beside her, Elmore's laughter faded. His smile dimmed into something more cautious as he noticed the way the crowd's eyes clung to them. He shifted uneasily, his glance darting toward Eliza.

"Maybe we should..." he murmured, almost under his breath.

Eliza cut him off with a bright, fearless smile. "Ignore them. Let them stare."

Her defiance lit something inside her—something untouchable.

Ann watched the exchange, her mouth twitching into a grin.

"Oh, let them gossip," she said cheerfully. "They'll find something else to talk about by supper."

Eliza laughed again, tipping her face up to the sun, refusing to let the weight of the world settle back onto her shoulders.

Elmore managed a small smile in return, though his fingers fidgeted with the edge of his coat as they continued walking together through the square.

Around them, whispers followed like ripples on water.

But for now, Eliza didn't hear them.

She only heard her own laughter—and the steady, hopeful beat of her heart.

♦ ♦ ♦ ♦ ♦ ♦

The walk back to Allendale was brisk, the winter sun sinking lower behind the trees. Eliza didn't mind. Her cheeks were still flushed from laughter, her heart lighter than it had been in months.

By the time she reached the front steps of the house, the world had begun to settle into the soft hush of late afternoon. She opened the door, a rush of warm air and the scent of woodsmoke greeting her.

She stepped inside, setting her small bag down carefully. As she unwound her shawl from around her shoulders, she caught movement out of the corner of her eye.

Across the foyer, John Allen stood in the doorway to the parlor. His figure was rigid, his face shadowed in the dim light spilling from the fire behind him.

"Eliza," he said, his voice low and weighted.

She paused, the last traces of her smile fading. Something in his tone chilled her far more than the winter air.

"Father?" she asked softly. "What is it?"

John didn't answer right away. He stepped aside instead, gesturing toward the parlor with a grave finality.

"Go into the parlor," he said.

Eliza hesitated, her heart beginning to thud heavily

against her ribs. She moved toward the room slowly, a knot of unease tightening inside her.

"It was only a matter of time before he came for me."

Eliza stepped into the parlor and stopped abruptly.

Sam stood near the fireplace, dressed impeccably in his formal attire, his tall frame casting a long shadow against the firelight. He turned at the sound of her entrance, his sharp eyes locking onto hers with a force that made her breath catch.

"Hello, Miss Eliza," he said softly, but there was steel in his voice.

Eliza's stomach churned, her earlier laughter now a distant memory. She grasped the doorframe tightly, the weight of his presence filling every inch of the room.

"Sam..." she said slowly, almost whispering.

His expression was serious, though a flicker of something—anger, disappointment, perhaps even hope—shifted beneath the surface.

Behind her, John lingered in the hallway, his face pale, watching.

Eliza closed the door softly behind her. She turned to face Sam fully, her hands clenched at her sides.

In his hand, he held her wedding ring, turning it over gently between his fingers, the gold catching the light with every movement. His face was strained, a man balancing pride against something far more fragile.

"I'm glad to see you, Eliza," he said, voice quiet.

Eliza said nothing. Her fingers twisted together as she watched him approach.

Sam took a step closer and held out the ring toward her.

"This belongs to you."

Eliza stared at the small band, her throat tightening. For a long, aching moment, she didn't move.

"I cannot accept it," she said at last, her voice barely more than a whisper.

Sam's hand dropped slightly, his grip tightening around the ring. He exhaled slowly, as if trying to steady the fury, or the grief, swelling inside him.

"Eliza, you're my wife," he said. "You're the First Lady of Tennessee."

His words were measured, almost pleading. But Eliza's gaze stayed firm, her resolve unshaken.

"My home is in Gallatin," she said quietly.

The words dropped between them like a stone.

Sam's jaw tightened. For a moment, his composure faltered. He forced a smile, but his voice wavered.

"Eliza, please. This... this will ruin me. My career, my reputation—everything I've worked for."

Eliza's expression softened, but she didn't move toward him.

"I'm sorry for that," she said gently. "Truly. But you and I... we were never meant to be."

Sam's face darkened with frustration. He stepped closer, desperation seeping into his voice.

"Do you know what you're throwing away? The General himself has assured me—I will be President, Eliza. You could be the First Lady of this nation. Think about what that means. Think about what it could mean for us."

Eliza's eyes shimmered, but she shook her head slowly.

"I have thought about it," she said, her voice breaking just slightly. "And I'm sorry, Sam... but I do not desire that life."

Sam stood frozen for a beat, the finality of her words crashing into him.

Slowly, he removed his own wedding band from his finger. He held it out to her, the gesture almost painful to watch.

"Then take this," he said, his voice raw.

Eliza stared at it but didn't reach for it.

"I can't," she said, her voice trembling.

The silence between them grew heavier with every breath.

Without another word, Sam turned toward the small table near the door. He placed the wedding ring down carefully, the soft clink of metal against wood echoing like a closing door.

Eliza's eyes fell to the ring, but she remained rooted in place.

Sam straightened, his words hollow but firm.

"Goodbye, Miss Eliza."

Without another glance at her, he crossed the room and stepped into the hall. His boots echoed against the hardwood as he left, the sound growing fainter until the door clicked shut behind him.

Eliza stood motionless, the fire crackling quietly in the hearth, the world outside silent and still.

She moved slowly to the window, pulling the curtain aside.

Outside, she watched as Sam's tall figure trudged down the long driveway, his coat billowing slightly in the cold breeze. He reached his horse, mounted it stiffly, and rode away without once looking back.

The sound of hooves faded into the distance.

Eliza let the curtain fall and turned away, her

shoulders sinking under the invisible weight pressing down on her. She sat heavily in the nearest chair, her hands limp in her lap, her gaze blank.

The ring gleamed softly from its place on the table, untouched, a final piece of a life she no longer wanted.

Present Day

Susie sat on the edge of the bed, her eyes wide with disbelief as she processed everything her mother had just told her.

Eliza leaned back against the pillows, looking smaller, worn by the weight of old memories.

"Being the First Lady," Eliza said softly, her voice almost a whisper, "was the last thing I wanted."
Susie swallowed hard, her voice trembling with curiosity.

"What happened to the ring?"
Eliza squinted, furrowing her brow as she tried to remember.

"If I recall," she said slowly, "I believe it's in the trunk."

Susie's gaze darted over to the trunk tucked in the corner of the room.

"And after he left..." Susie began, her voice hesitant, "what became of him?"

Eliza gave a short chuckle, but there was no joy in it—only a tired sort of sadness.

"He went back to Nashville," she said. "But not as the man he was before."

For a moment, the room fell silent. Susie sat still, waiting, sensing that there was more her mother wasn't saying—more that perhaps couldn't be said at all.

And across the room, the old trunk sat silently in the corner, holding pieces of a life Susie was only just beginning to understand.

Resignation

March 3, 1829, Gallatin, Tennessee

The bar at the Nashville Inn was dimly lit, the air thick with the mingled scents of whiskey and tobacco. Laughter and conversation buzzed low among the patrons—until the door creaked open.

Sam Houston stepped inside.

The room quieted almost instantly. A few men whispered behind their hands; others smirked openly.

Sam's shoulders sagged under the weight of his problems. His face, once so commanding, was hollow now.

At the far end of the bar, Sheriff Willoughby Williams caught sight of him and waved him over.

"Sam! Where have you been all day? General Hall's been tearing his hair out trying to wrangle votes in the Senate."

Houston barely acknowledged him. He slumped into the seat across from Willoughby without a word.

"Did you hear me?" Willoughby pressed, leaning forward.

Slowly, Sam looked up. His face was drawn, his eyes bloodshot and empty.

"I heard you," Sam said. His voice was flat, hollow. "General Hall... he has bigger concerns now."

Willoughby frowned, confused. "What's that supposed to mean?"

Sam didn't answer. Instead, he pushed back from the table abruptly and motioned for Willoughby to follow him.

The hallway of the Nashville Inn was dim and narrow, the floorboards creaking under their boots. A smoky haze hung in the air from the taproom below. Sam moved down the hall without speaking, his steps heavy and determined, his coat brushing the walls in the tight space.

Willoughby followed closely behind, confusion knitting his brow.

At the end of the hall, Sam climbed the narrow staircase, his hand trailing along the chipped banister. Willoughby hesitated for a moment at the base of the stairs, then hurried after him, his heart pounding in his chest.

Sam pushed open the door to his room, and Willoughby stepped into a space that looked like it had weathered a storm.

Torn scraps of paper littered the floor and the desk, the remnants of a letter shredded in a moment of fury.

Sam crossed to the desk and sank heavily into the chair, his broad shoulders slumped as if the very act of sitting took the last of his strength.

Without a word, he pulled out a clean sheet of paper and dipped his pen into the inkwell with mechanical precision.

Willoughby stood by the door, glancing at the wreckage scattered around the room, unease gnawing at him.

As Sam began to write, his voice seemed to fill the room—not aloud, but deep within the memory, carried by the sinking weight of regret.

"It has become my duty to resign the office of Chief Magistrate of the state," Sam wrote, the pen scratching steadily against the paper, "and to place in your hands the authority and responsibility which, on such an event, devolves on you by the provisions of our Constitution."

Willoughby watched, his disbelief growing with every line.

Sam's hand remained steady even as the rest of him seemed to crumble inward.

"In dissolving the political connection which has so long, and in such a variety of forms, existed between the people of Tennessee and myself," the words flowed from him with grim finality, "no private affliction, however deep or incurable, can forbid an expression of the grateful recollections due to the kindness and partialities of an indulgent public."

When he finished, Sam set the pen down carefully, as if any sudden movement might shatter what little remained of him.

"Finished," he said tightly, without looking up.

He folded the letter with deliberate precision, sealed it, and pressed it into the sheriff's hands.

"Take this to General Hall," Sam said. "Tell him he's the governor now."

Willoughby stared at the letter, then back at Sam, his face drawn and alarmed.

"Sam, you don't have to do this," he said urgently. "A failed marriage—people will talk, sure, but they'll move on. You can still lead."

Sam rose slowly from his chair, his broad frame seeming to shrink with every breath he took. His hollow eyes locked onto Willoughby's.

"I am a ruined man," Sam said simply. "I exonerate her fully. I don't justify myself... I shall go into exile."

Willoughby shook his head, desperate for words that would change his friend's mind. But Sam extended his hand.

Reluctantly, Willoughby reached out and shook it.

"Goodbye, Willoughby," Sam said quietly. "You've been a loyal friend."

Willoughby swallowed hard, nodded once, and tucked the letter carefully under his coat. Without another word, he turned and left, the door closing softly behind him.

Sam stood alone.

The silence pressed in from all sides, thick and suffocating.

He moved slowly across the room, pouring himself a glass of whiskey from the decanter on the sideboard. The amber liquid swirled in the glass, catching the firelight in fleeting glimmers.

Sam stood by the window, staring out at the lights across the city.

He swirled the drink in his hand for a long moment, feeling the full, crushing weight of everything he had lost.

Then, with a slow, resigned motion, he raised the glass to his lips and took a long, burning sip—staring into a future he no longer recognized.

◆ ◆ ◆ ◆ ◆ ◆

The following morning, the sun reflected sharply off the Cumberland River. The bustling docks were alive with the noise of workers shouting, crates being unloaded, and the hiss of steam from arriving riverboats.

Among the crowd, a strange figure stood awkwardly near the gangplank—a tall man, bundled in a woman's ill-fitting shawl and bonnet.

Sam Houston shifted uneasily, his towering frame unmistakable even under the flimsy disguise. Passersby paused to stare, some snickering openly. Dockworkers elbowed each other, pointing and laughing.

Sam tugged the shawl tighter around his face, his broad shoulders hunched forward as if he could somehow make himself smaller.

"He disguised himself as a woman and boarded a steamboat," Eliza said softly, her voice thick with a complicated sadness.

Sam shuffled awkwardly toward the gangplank, ignoring the muffled laughter that followed him.

His eyes darted around, scanning the dock for any sign of trouble, any sign of someone who might recognize him.

A small group of dockhands hooted in mockery as he passed, but no one stepped forward to challenge him.

With a final tug of the bonnet to shield his face, Sam boarded the steamboat. A few passengers gawked as he shuffled onto the deck, but the bustle of river travel soon swallowed him.

"He fled to Arkansas," Eliza's voice continued, laced with a mixture of pity and inevitability, "With nowhere else to go he returned to the only people who had ever accepted him without question — the Cherokee."

The steamboat's whistle shrieked, a high, mournful sound that echoed across the frozen river.

The gangplank was pulled away. Ropes were loosed. The great paddlewheel churned the water into a frothy wake.

Sam stood near the railing, gripping the wood so tightly his knuckles turned white. He stared down into the swirling current, the cold wind tugging at his ridiculous shawl.

Behind him, Nashville receded—its spires and rooftops growing smaller.

Sam Houston did not look back.

Rebirth

April 25, 1829, Arkansas Territory

The interior of the teepee was dim, lit only by the faint glow of a small fire in the center. Smoke curled lazily toward the open vent above.

Sam Houston sat slumped against the hide wall, dressed in traditional Cherokee garb. His clothing hung askew on his frame, the beads and leather dulled with wear. A half-empty bottle of whiskey dangled from his limp fingers.

His eyes were bloodshot, his face unshaven, the proud governor of Tennessee reduced to a broken man.

The flap of the teepee rustled, and Oolooteka entered, the elder's movements sure and deliberate. He stopped short when he caught sight of Sam, and his expression soured into disappointment.

"Look at you," Oolooteka said, his voice laced with disgust.

Sam groaned, but didn't lift his head. He took another swig from the bottle, the liquor dribbling slightly from the corner of his mouth.

Oolooteka stepped closer, the firelight catching in his hard eyes.

"The Great Raven," he said bitterly, "reduced to this?"

The words cut deep, though Sam gave no outward sign beyond a faint flinch.

"The Cherokee had once called him Colonneh — the raven," Eliza's voice said softly, her words full of old sorrow.

Houston gritted his teeth but didn't look up.

Oolooteka's voice hardened.

"Sam, stand up. There's someone here to see you."

At first, Sam didn't move. Then the teepee flap stirred again, and a figure entered—a young woman, her presence filling the dim space with something lighter, warmer.

Diana.

Now in her twenties, Diana had grown into a striking woman, her long dark hair braided neatly over one shoulder. Her eyes, full of intelligence and kindness, found Sam immediately.

Houston's eyes widened, and for the first time in what felt like months, he smiled.

"Diana!" he said, his voice cracking with emotion.

He scrambled awkwardly to his feet, nearly dropping the bottle. He fumbled to smooth his wrinkled clothing, ran a clumsy hand through his tangled hair, trying to pull himself together in her presence.

"It's wonderful to see you," he said, his voice softer now, trembling with something that might have been hope.

Diana smiled at him—a small, patient smile—but behind it was a glimmer of pity.

"He found companionship in Diana," Eliza's voice continued, low and steady. "A young woman who had once admired him as a girl. Before long, they were married, and he tried to rebuild his life among the Cherokee."

Sam stood there, swaying slightly, blinking against the firelight as Diana crossed to him.

And for a moment—just a moment—the great raven, battered and broken, seemed to find his wings again.

Present Day

Eliza watched the fire, her voice soft but laden with memory. "Sam fled to the Cherokee, a broken man. But Diana, who'd known him as a boy, saw something worth saving. They married, ran a store, and for a time, he found purpose again, brokering treaties with the same charm that once swayed Tennessee. But it wasn't enough to hold him. It wasn't long before he was in Washington meeting with the General and other politicians on behalf of the Cherokee."

Susie sat forward on the edge of the bed, her eyes wide, her hands curled tightly in her lap. "So, you both just... moved on?" she asked, her voice full of disbelief.

Eliza frowned, her gaze drifting to the flames as old wounds stirred. "Not exactly," she said softly. "The Democratic Party ruled Tennessee politics then, and when Sam went west, many were furious—demanding a pound of flesh."

Susie leaned closer, her heart thudding. "What happened?"

Eliza sighed. "People whispered about me, blamed me. Some said worse. Then one day, a letter came—a subpoena, summoning me to the courthouse here in town."

Susie's mouth fell open in shock.

"They wanted me to defend myself," Eliza said, her voice trembling. "As if leaving him was a crime."

She shook her head, the firelight catching the silver in her hair. "I thought it ridiculous, but Father—your grandfather—took it seriously."

Susie stared at her mother, seeing her in a way she never had before—not just as a parent, but as a woman who had endured the impossible.

And Eliza, lost in the long shadows of her past, could almost feel the cold weight of that letter in her daughter's hands once more.

December 14, 1831, Washington D. C.

The marble halls of the Capitol echoed with the sharp clack of boots against stone. Sam Houston, towering and unmistakable even in a strange mix of buckskin and Native attire, strode through the corridors with purpose. His long coat swung at his heels, and despite his disheveled appearance, heads turned to watch him pass.

From a side hall, Robert Allen emerged, his face tight with urgency. He caught Sam's arm and pulled him aside.

"Sam, they're trying to ruin Eliza," Robert said in a low, hurried voice. "They've got her on trial in Sumner County, calling her virtue into question."

Sam's expression darkened, a storm brewing behind his tired eyes.

"They'll listen to you," Robert pressed. "If you write a letter, it might stop this nonsense."

For a moment, Sam hesitated. He fought through the conflicting emotions flashing across his face.

"This is a witch hunt, Sam. Please... You swore to me you'd protect her!"

Sam nodded once, sharp and certain. He dropped into a chair at a small writing desk nearby and snatched up a pen. Without ceremony, he began to write, his hand steady, his face grim with focus.

"He was in Washington to speak on behalf of the Cherokee," Eliza whispered, steady and low, "but he stopped long enough to write a letter – one that would clear my name."

When he finished, Sam folded the letter and pressed it firmly into Robert's hand.

"Thank you, Sam," Robert said, scanning the page quickly and nodding in gratitude.

Sam stood, clasping Robert's hand with quiet strength.

"Please give her mother and father my warmest regards."

January 10, 1832, Gallatin, Tennessee

The Sumner County courthouse was thick with murmurs and the rustle of stiff suits as men packed the benches and aisles. The air was heavy with judgment and something meaner still—curiosity.

John Allen entered through the front doors, his face drawn tight with anger and fear. In his hand, he clutched the letter like a lifeline.

He stepped forward, facing the gathered men, and raised his voice to cut through the din.

"Gentlemen," he said, steady despite the pounding of his heart. "I have here a letter from Governor Houston. If you'll allow me, I'll read it."

The room fell abruptly silent. Dozens of eyes turned toward him, suspicion and interest sharpening the air.

John unfolded the letter carefully and cleared his throat.

"'Mr. Allen, whatever had been my feelings or opinions in relation to Eliza at one time, I have been satisfied.'"

A ripple of shock moved through the room.

John read on, his voice growing stronger.

"'If mortal man had dared to charge Eliza or say aught against her virtue, I would have slain him. That I have and do love Eliza, none can doubt.'"

Men shifted in their seats, exchanging glances. The weight of Sam Houston's words pressed down on the room.

John's voice softened slightly as he reached the final lines.

"'Eliza stands acquitted by me. I have received her

as a virtuous wife, and as such, I pray to God I may ever regard her. My future happiness can only exist in the assurance that Eliza and myself can be happy. You can forget the past and forgive all.'"

John folded the letter with deliberate care, the paper crackling in the hush.

Before he could step away, Judge Jocephus Conn Guild — one of the most respected men in the county — rose slowly from his seat near the front.

"May I see that letter, Mr. Allen?" he asked.

John hesitated for only a moment before stepping forward and handing the folded page to him.

Guild opened the letter carefully. He skimmed the words in silence, his brow furrowing slightly as he read. The room held its breath, the air charged with anticipation.

Finally, he looked up, his expression grave.

"This is Sam's handwriting," he said, his voice low but firm. He held the letter up for the others to see, a silent confirmation. "It is settled."

A murmur of agreement rippled through the room. Heads nodded, the last embers of gossip and judgment smothered by the finality of Sam Houston's words.

"Sam could have said a thousand awful things," Eliza recounted. "Most of them true... Instead, he saved me. It cleared my name, but it still took several years to finalize the divorce, since he was in another state."

John Allen tucked the letter back into his coat, his chest swelling with relief. He offered a short, respectful nod to Guild, then turned and walked briskly from the courthouse.

Present Day

Susie sat motionless on the edge of the bed, her eyes wide, her hands tangled in the folds of her skirt.

"He really wrote that?" she asked, her voice full of wonder.

Eliza nodded slowly, her voice soft but steady.

"He didn't have to," she said. "But he did. And for that, I'll always be grateful."

Susie leaned back, her mind turning over everything she had just heard, trying to fit the legend of Sam Houston with the broken, human pieces her mother had shown her. A moment passed before she spoke again.

"He may have been The Big Drunk," Susie said thoughtfully, "but he wasn't all bad, was he?"

Eliza smiled faintly, her gaze wandering toward the flickering firelight.

"No, Susie," she said. "He wasn't all bad. Not at all. He was an honorable man."

The two women sat in silence for a long moment, the past and present weaving together between them, stitched by the soft rhythm of the fire and the quiet, aching truth of a story almost forgotten.

Revolution

April 13, 1833, San Felipe de Austin, Texas

In a cramped meeting room filled with smoke and tension, Sam Houston stood at the head of a rough-hewn table. Around him gathered a mix of white men in frontier suits and Hispanic men in formal attire, their faces lined with worry and expectation. The air was thick with the scent of tobacco and sweat.

A large map was spread across the table, weighed down at the corners with ink pots and knives. Sam leaned over it, his finger tracing bold, deliberate movements across the parchment as he spoke, the words carrying to every corner of the room.

Beside him stood Stephen F. Austin, his expression grave, his hands clasped tightly behind his back. Austin nodded now and then, his silent presence lending weight to every word Sam uttered.

"We must draft a constitution," Sam said firmly, his finger tapping a spot on the map. "One that will show Mexico we desire to remain loyal — if they will recognize Texas as a separate state within their republic."

Murmurs of agreement rippled through the room.

Sam straightened, his eyes sweeping across the gathered men.

"We petition Mexico for statehood. We offer peace. But we also prepare," he said, his voice steeling. "In case they refuse us."

At his side, Austin gave a somber nod.

Eliza's voice, steady and thoughtful, threaded through the memory. "He was in Texas with the Cherokee around the time Mr. Austin petitioned the Mexican government for statehood. Tensions boiled over, sparking the Texas Revolution. Being the soldier he was, Sam couldn't resist the call to lead."

Sam pulled a sheet of parchment toward him, his pen flying across the surface as he drafted the letter. His words were sharp, clear, and unwavering call to unity and vigilance.

The men around the table leaned in, their faces drawn with hope and fear alike.

Even with letters, petitions and carefully worded pleas, the storm was coming.

Out in the wide, open fields of Texas, the sun blazed hot against the dusty earth. A ragtag army — barely more than farmers, blacksmiths, and shopkeepers — moved through clumsy drills, their muskets clutched in calloused hands.

Sam Houston stood before them, his posture tall and unyielding. His buckskin jacket was worn and battered, his hat pulled low against the sun, but there was a fire in his eyes that even defeat could not extinguish.

He moved among his men, calling out corrections, steadying a nervous hand here, adjusting a musket grip there. Every ounce of his will was bent toward shaping them into something stronger than the enemy believed possible. They were not trained soldiers. But under Sam's steady leadership, they would become an army.

March 7, 1836, San Antonio

Beyond the training grounds, the reality of war loomed large.

Only a few weeks earlier, tensions between the settlers of Texas and the Mexican government had exploded into open rebellion. What had begun as a petition for self-rule had become a bloody struggle for independence. The settlers—Tejanos and Americans alike—wanted freedom. Mexico's dictator, General Antonio López de Santa Anna, would give them only submission.

The Alamo stood as a silent, ruined testament to the cost of that defiance.

Under the cover of night, the once-proud fort smoldered. Smoke curled from its blackened walls, twisting into the dark Texas sky. The bodies of nearly two hundred Texan defenders lay scattered across the blood-soaked ground—heroes whose sacrifice would never be forgotten.

"After the fall of the Alamo," Eliza's voice continued softly, *"Sam knew he couldn't engage Santa Anna's army—not yet. He didn't have the numbers."*

Atop a black horse, Santa Anna surveyed the destruction with cold satisfaction. His small frame belied the force of his ambition. The Mexican flag snapped triumphantly above the battered mission, a brutal warning to all who would resist him.

"Since Sam kept falling back, Santa Anna grew frustrated. He wanted a swift end to the Revolution. So he

made a mistake."

Susie leaned closer, hanging onto every word as her mother spoke.

"Santa Anna split his forces and sent them to kill Mr. Austin and the other elected members of the Texas government," Eliza continued. "He thought Sam was scared. He thought we would run."

But Sam Houston was not beaten.

He was waiting.

Learning of Santa Anna's plans, Sam moved swiftly on the smaller army led by Santa Anna. He led his men across rivers and through marshes, pushing them hard, molding them for one chance—one decisive strike that could change everything.

The embers of the Alamo still smoldered in the darkness, but somewhere beyond the horizon, in the wild heart of Texas, Sam Houston was preparing to strike back.

The Revolution was not over.

April 21, 1836, La Porte, Texas

The midday sun beat down on a bluff where two Texan scouts lay hidden among the brush. Below them, in the wide, flat clearing near the San Jacinto River, the Mexican army had made camp.

Thin tendrils of smoke rose from smoldering campfires. Horses wandered lazily among the scattered tents. And the soldiers—hundreds of them—were sprawled out on the ground, their weapons tossed carelessly aside, their bodies exhausted from days of marching.

One scout shifted his weight carefully, peering through the tall grass.

"They're all asleep," he whispered, disbelief thick in his voice.

Beside him, the second scout nodded grimly, his eyes wide with urgency.

"Quickly! We must alert General Houston."

They slid back from the edge of the bluff and sprinted for their horses, their boots kicking up clouds of dust. Swinging into the saddles, they drove the tired animals hard, thundering across the open land toward the Texan encampment.

"At San Jacinto," Eliza said, "Sam's scouts discovered the Mexican army taking a siesta."

Across the field at the Texan army's campsite, Sam Houston stood with his officers gathered loosely around him, the spring breeze tugging at the edges of their coats.

The thundering hooves of the approaching scouts broke the stillness. Dust trailed behind the riders as they pulled up sharply, swinging down before Sam with barely a moment's hesitation.

"They're all sleeping, sir," one scout gasped, still catching his breath. "Santa Anna's men—over a thousand of them—stretched out by the river. Their guns piled up. No guards posted."

Sam's eyes narrowed, processing the words quickly. He looked out toward the horizon, toward where the enemy lay vulnerable and unready.

"Seizing the opportunity," Eliza recounted. "Sam rallied his men for an attack."

The camp exploded into motion. Muskets were primed, powder horns checked, bayonets fastened with trembling hands. Orders were barked out, boots pounding against the earth. Some men prayed under their breath; others tightened their hands around their rifles and knives.

Sam moved among them like a force of nature, steadying the uncertain, driving the bold, his very presence fanning the spark of desperation into the fire of purpose.

This was the moment he had waited for.

And he would not let it pass.

◆ ◆ ◆ ◆ ◆ ◆

With a roar, hundreds of Texan soldiers surged out from the woods and across the open prairie toward the Mexican camp at San Jacinto. The battle cries of "Remember the Alamo!" ripped through the air, each shout a promise of vengeance.

Sam Houston led the charge himself, sword gleaming in the sunlight, his horse pounding forward as dust rose in thick clouds behind him.

Below the bluff, the Mexican soldiers — still drowsy from their siesta — scrambled in confusion. Officers shouted desperate orders, but the men were caught off guard, their weapons stacked far from reach. Some stumbled barefoot across the trampled grass, half-dressed and unarmed, as the Texans closed in.

Gunfire erupted. The first shots cracked through the air, muskets blazing from the Texan line with ruthless precision. Men fell where they stood. The smell of black powder burned the wind.

Santa Anna's forces tried to rally, but it was too late.

Texan cavalry swung wide around the flanks, cutting off any hope of retreat. Infantrymen surged over the camp, bayonets flashing, cutting down those who resisted. The battle turned to chaos and slaughter in moments.

The Mexican army — veterans who had crushed resistance at the Alamo — crumbled under the ferocity of the assault.

"It was a rout," Eliza recalled through the haze of memory.

Within just eighteen minutes, the battle was over.

Bodies lay scattered among the smoldering campfires. Muskets and sabers littered the bloodstained ground. Texans captured hundreds of prisoners while others fled blindly into the nearby marshes, their boots sinking into the muddy earth as they threw down their weapons and begged for mercy.

Sam Houston reined in his horse at the center of the captured camp. His leg had been shattered by a musket ball during the assault, but he stayed mounted, refusing to show weakness to his men — or to history.

"Take prisoners," he commanded, his voice rough but steady. "The slaughter is finished."

Texan soldiers fanned out across the marshes and woods, hunting the survivors who had fled. Among the prisoners dragged back to camp was a man in a torn uniform, caked with mud and trembling from fear and exhaustion.

At first, few recognized him.

But soon, a shout went up.

It was Santa Anna.

Gone was the proud general in gleaming uniform. Now he wore the tattered disguise of an ordinary soldier's clothes, his face hollow, his dignity stripped bare. He clutched his hat in both hands, his head bowed low.

The soldiers shoved him forward roughly.

Santa Anna stumbled, then straightened, forcing his eyes upward. His dark eyes met Sam's across the distance — pleading, desperate, defeated.

"Sam was shot in the ankle during the battle, but he survived, said Eliza. "When Santa Anna was captured, it was the end of the revolution. Sam was hailed as the savior of Texas."

Battered and broken but unbowed, Sam accepted Santa Anna's surrender.

Victory.
And with it, a new nation was born.
Texas was free.

October 22, 1836, Columbia, Texas

The courthouse bustled with energy, the grand room filled beyond capacity. Men packed the aisles and stood shoulder-to-shoulder along the walls. Rough settlers in worn buckskins stood alongside polished politicians in pressed suits. Veterans of San Jacinto, some still bearing the scars of battle, their faces alight with pride.

At the front of the room, a platform had been erected, draped modestly in the colors of the new Republic—red, white, and blue. A single Bible rested on a podium, its worn leather binding a quiet testament to the gravity of the day.

Sam Houston stepped forward.

He leaned slightly on a cane, his ankle still tender from the wound he'd carried off the field at San Jacinto, but his posture was straight, his chin lifted.

The room fell into a reverent silence as he approached the podium.

He placed his right hand firmly on the Bible, the murmur of the crowd dying completely away.

A judge, robed and solemn, intoned the oath of office.

Sam's voice, deep and steady, carried across the packed room.

"I, Samuel Houston, do solemnly swear that I will faithfully execute the duties of the office of President of the Republic of Texas... and will, to the best of my ability, preserve, protect, and defend the Constitution and laws of this Republic."

As he finished, the judge nodded gravely and extended his hand.

The room erupted in thunderous applause.

Men cheered, their hats tossed into the air. Some wept openly. Others pounded their fists against the walls in celebration. The noise shook the very rafters of the courthouse.

Full of awe and sadness, Eliza's voice cut through the memory. "He became the first President of the Republic of Texas. The man who had once fled Tennessee in disgrace had built a new nation."

Sam turned to the crowd, offering a brief, humble nod, his hand still resting lightly on the Bible for a moment longer.

He did not smile.

There was pride in his bearing, but not triumph. Too many ghosts stood with him in that room — ghosts from the Alamo, from a long road paved with sacrifice.

He knew better than anyone the true cost of the moment.

Outside the courthouse, church bells rang out across the town. The sound carried on the Texas wind, reaching across fields and rivers and into the hearts of a fledgling nation.

For the first time, Texas was not a dream.

It was real.

Present Day

Susie sat perched on the edge of the bed, her face alight with wonder.

"You were the First Lady of Texas?" she asked, her voice hushed in amazement.

Eliza smiled faintly, the lines at the corners of her mouth deepening.

"Technically, yes," she said. "Our divorce wasn't finalized until after Sam had already taken office."

Susie leaned back slightly, trying to process the weight of what she had just learned. The enormity of her mother's hidden history seemed almost too large to fit inside the small, firelit room.

"So... if you hadn't left him," Susie said slowly, a playful glint in her eye, "Texas might still belong to Mexico?"

Eliza let out a soft laugh, the sound warm and a little wistful.

"I suppose it would," she said, her voice teasing but touched with truth.

For a moment, they shared a smile — light cutting through the memories. But then Susie's curiosity deepened, and she tilted her head, her voice gentler.

Eliza sat quietly, staring into the fire. The crackle and pop of the wood filled the silence as her thoughts wandered back through the long corridor of years.

After a moment, she spoke, her words emerging quietly, reflective.

"If I had stayed with him... if I had been the kind of wife he wanted me to be..." She paused, her eyes distant. "Sam would have been President of the United States."

Susie blinked in disbelief.

"Really?" she whispered.

Eliza turned her head slowly to meet her daughter's wide eyes. Her voice was calm, almost matter-of-fact.

"Yes," she said simply. "I have no doubt of it."

She leaned back slightly against the pillows, gathering her strength before continuing.

"Mr. Polk—James K. Polk—was a nice enough man, but he was a very unpopular governor. He was voted out after only one term. He would have faded into history without much note."

Susie listened intently, her lips parted in wonder.

"The General," Eliza said, meaning Andrew Jackson, "was a kingmaker in those days. After Mr. Van Buren faltered at the Convention, he championed Mr. Polk. He made a deal with party leaders vowing only one term and placed him in the Executive Mansion. Without Jackson's blessing, Polk would have never reached the presidency."

Eliza gave a small shrug, the weight of inevitability in her voice.

"If Sam had stayed governor, if he hadn't fled west... Jackson would have chosen him instead."

Susie shook her head slowly, struggling to take it all in.

"I can't believe it," she said, her voice filled with awe. "You could have been First Lady of the whole country."

Eliza smiled faintly, a mixture of humor and sadness flickering across her face.

"But I wouldn't have been happy, Susie," she said. "Not for a moment."

The fire snapped sharply in the hearth, and for a

time they sat in silence, the past and all its might-have-beens stretching out between them.

Finally, Susie asked, her voice quieter, more hesitant.

"Did you ever see him again?"

Eliza's smile faded, her gaze turning inward, the memory stirring once more.

Forgiveness

August 16, 1844, Lebanon, Tennessee

The sticky heat of late summer clung to Cedar Grove Cemetery like a wet blanket.

Mourners in black stood beneath the sweltering sun, their faces flushed and somber, handkerchiefs pressed constantly to their foreheads. Grief hung just as thickly in the air as the heat.

Today, they laid Congressman Robert Allen to rest—Eliza's beloved uncle.

Near the front of the burial plot, Presidents Andrew Jackson and James K. Polk moved slowly through the crowd. Jackson, now gaunt and hunched with age, leaned heavily on a cane, his steps deliberate and pained. The deep lines of his face were carved with the weariness of too many years and too many battles, both public and private.

They stopped to shake John Allen's hand, offering quiet condolences beneath the glaring sun.

Off to the side, shaded beneath a drooping oak, Eliza stood alone. She clutched her shawl loosely around her elbows, though it offered little comfort from the heat. She didn't notice the familiar presence until it was almost beside her.

"Good afternoon, Miss Eliza," came a voice she hadn't heard in years.

Startled, she turned.

For a moment, she was frozen, staring as if at a ghost.

Sam Houston stood there, older but no less

striking. His dark hair was streaked with gray, and there was a deeper heaviness about his eyes now—a gravity earned not just through battlefields, but through the slow, bruising toll of time.

He removed his hat respectfully, his gaze steady but softened.

"Please accept my condolences," he said. "Your uncle was a good friend. I am going to miss him."

Eliza swallowed, willing her voice to rise above the lump in her throat.

"Thank you," she said quietly. "I will too."

They stood for a long moment in the shaded hush, the world spinning on without them.

Sam studied her with a small, almost wistful smile.

"You look lovely as always," he said gently. "I trust you are well?"

Eliza managed a tentative smile in return, though her heart ached with the weight of what had been and what could never be.

"Yes," she said. Her voice steadied as she added, "I hear you've had quite the success in Texas."

Sam chuckled lightly, the sound warm but tinged with sorrow.

"Yes," he said. "It's been quite the adventure."

A silence stretched between them, thick, but not cruel.

Eliza hesitated, then stepped closer, speaking from the heart.

"Sam... I'm sorry. I'm sorry for it all."

His expression softened further, his dark eyes kind.

"There's nothing to be sorry for," he said simply.

From across the cemetery, Andrew Jackson's voice rasped through the air.

"Sam!" he called, his cane thudding sharply against the dry ground as he waved him over impatiently.

Sam glanced toward the General, then turned back to Eliza, bowing his head respectfully.

"Excuse me, Miss Eliza. It was nice to see you."

He turned to leave, but something inside Eliza broke free.

"Sam," she said, her voice trembling but clear. He paused, surprised, and turned.

Without a second thought, she crossed the small distance between them and threw her arms around him.

Sam stiffened for a breathless moment, stunned by her touch, and then, slowly, almost reverently, returned her embrace. His arms tightened around her, drawing her into the deep, steady rhythm of his heartbeat.

She clung to him for a long moment, breathing him in—dust, heat, leather, and something still fiercely, achingly familiar.

When they finally pulled apart, Sam's eyes glistened. So did hers.

Jackson's cane rapped again with impatient authority behind them.

"Sam, are you ready?" he called, his voice thinning under the strain of age.

Sam cleared his throat and nodded.

"Yes, General," he answered.

With one final smile, Sam turned and walked away beside Jackson, his tall figure slowly swallowed by the shimmering heat rising off the cemetery grounds.

Eliza stood unmoving beneath the drooping oak.

Tears slid down her cheeks—not tears of bitterness, nor even regret.

In that brief, stolen moment beneath the August sun, there had been forgiveness.

There had been peace.

A Happy Ending

Present Day

The fire crackled low, casting a soft glow across the worn quilt and the lines of Eliza's face.

She sat quietly for a moment, wiping her eyes with a handkerchief as she finished her story. Across from her, Susie blinked rapidly, but a solitary tear escaped and traced a shining path down her cheek.

Without hesitation, Susie reached out and took her mother's hands, her fingers curling gently around them.

Eliza smiled warmly and, with trembling fingers, reached up and wiped the tear from her daughter's face.

"Oh dear," she said softly, her voice thick with tenderness, "this is not a sad story."

She gave Susie's hands a little squeeze.

"I had quite the happy ending."

A wide grin spread across Eliza's face as she leaned back against the pillows.

For a moment, she said nothing — only sat there smiling, her mind wafting back across the years.

Through all the heartbreak, through all the trouble, Eliza found herself remembering not the pain, but the laughter. The love. The second chances that had come when she least expected them.

And for the first time in hours, the room felt lighter.

The past was not a burden here.

It was a part of her — a testament to how far she had come, and to all the joy she had found after letting go of what was never meant to be.

June 3, 1840, Gallatin, Tennessee

The sun shone brightly over the little church on the square, bathing the town in a golden warmth.

Eliza, radiant in a simple but elegant wedding dress, walked hand-in-hand with Elmore down the steps of the church. The gathered crowd cheered, their voices rising joyously into the cloudless sky. Fists full of rice sailed through the air, the tiny grains glinting in the sunlight like a shower of stars.

"I have lived a wonderful life," Eliza's voice said softly.

Elmore beamed down at her, his expression full of pride and love, while Eliza's laughter rang out clear and sweet, filling the space between them.

March 26, 1843, Gallatin, Tennessee

Music filled the sitting room, the joyful strains of Elmore's fiddle weaving around the furniture like a living thing.

Seated in the corner, Elmore tapped his foot in rhythm as he played, a lively tune dancing from the strings beneath his fingers.

"I got to spend it with you and your father," Eliza's voice said, filled with warmth.

In the center of the room, a two-year-old Susie spun in clumsy circles, her tiny feet stomping with delight, her giggles a high, bubbling counterpoint to the music.

Eliza laughed so hard she tumbled right out of her chair, sprawling onto the floor, her dress pooling around her like a puddle. Her laughter echoed off the walls, mingling with the music and the peals of her daughter's happiness.

Present Day

The fire in the hearth burned low, casting a soft, amber glow across the quiet room.

Elmore entered, moving with slow, careful steps, a glass of water in his hand. His face, weathered by years of simple, honest living, softened with love as he crossed to Eliza's side.

"You haven't had much water today," he said gently.

Eliza smiled up at him, tired but grateful, and took the glass with trembling hands.

"Thank you, Elmore."

He stood there for a moment, watching her with concern.

"Is there anything you need?" he asked.

Eliza gazed at him, her smile deepening with an affection that even time could not dim.

"You've already given me everything," she said, her voice breaking with emotion. "You gave me the life I always wanted."

Her hands tightened slightly around the glass, her heart swelling with gratitude.

"The good Lord truly blessed me."

Elmore nodded, swallowing thickly. He leaned down, brushing a tender kiss across her forehead, then turned and shuffled quietly toward the door.

Eliza watched him go, her smile faltering as a quiet resolve settled over her.

Turning her attention to Susie, who sat silently at the foot of the bed, Eliza gathered her strength.

"Susie," she said, her voice firmer.

Startled, Susie looked up, noticing the shift in her

mother's demeanor.

"There is something I need your help with."

"Whatever you need, Momma."

Eliza's hand trembled as she gestured weakly toward the portrait hanging on the wall—a painting that captured her in youth, all bright eyes and dreams not yet broken.

"When I'm gone," Eliza said, "I want you to burn my portraits. All of them."

Susie's mouth fell open, horror spreading across her face.

"Momma!"

Eliza's gaze drifted to the trunk at the foot of the bed.

"The letter too," she added.

Susie shook her head in confusion.

"Why?" she whispered.

Eliza's voice was calm, unyielding.

"People still talk about Sam and me. I won't leave anything behind to tarnish his legacy. No grave marker either."

Susie stared at her, struggling to grasp the weight of what her mother was asking. Finally, she nodded, her voice quiet and full of emotion.

"I'll take care of it."

Eliza's face softened, a deep peace settling over her.

"Thank you, my darling girl."

Susie reached out and took her mother's frail hand, holding it tightly between her own.

Eliza's body shuddered slightly as a fit of coughing shook her, and Susie leaned forward quickly, adjusting the blanket around her shoulders.

"Rest, Momma," she whispered.

Eliza closed her eyes, her breathing slow but steady. The fire cracked gently in the hearth as the room fell into a profound, reverent silence — broken only by the quiet rustle of Susie's movements as she kept watch by her mother's side.

Outside the window, the night deepened, wrapping the world in stillness.

"Goodbye, Momma"

March 6, 1861, Gallatin, Tennessee

The bedroom was silent, save for the faint crackling of the low fire in the hearth.

Once filled with laughter and warmth, the space now felt cold and abandoned, the shadows longer, the air heavier. Dust clung to the corners of the room, and the once-bright fabrics had dulled.

Dressed in mourning black, Susie stood in the doorway, her heart pounding.

Elmore remained beside her, his hand gentle on her shoulder.

"Take all the time you need," he said softly.

Susie nodded, her throat tight with unshed tears. She pressed briefly against him, taking comfort in his steady presence.

"I'll be down in a few minutes," she whispered.

Elmore gave her arm a gentle squeeze, then quietly slipped out of the room, leaving her alone.

Susie stepped inside, each footstep sounding loud against the wooden floor. Her eyes moved slowly around the space—the shawl draped across the rocking chair, the Bible resting on the nightstand, the faint scent of lavender still in the air.

Her eyes caught on the portrait hanging on the wall.

She crossed to it, her steps steady but reluctant, and lifted it down carefully.

She cradled it against her chest for a long moment, blinking back tears.

"You told me to burn it..." she whispered.

Her fingers trembled as she carried the portrait to the fire.

For a heartbeat, she hesitated. The painted image of her mother as a young lady smiled serenely at her through the wavering light.

Susie swallowed hard, then, with a deep breath, she pitched the portrait into the flames.

The fire swiftly consumed the canvas. The oil bubbled and blackened, the image of Eliza disappearing into smoke and ash.

Susie turned away, her hands shaking.

She knelt before the trunk at the foot of the bed and lifted the lid. Layers of her mother's belongings were tucked inside—gloves, scarves, old letters tied neatly with ribbon.

She dug through them until her hand closed around the letter.

Sam's letter.

Tears filled her eyes as she held it over the fire.

For a moment, she nearly faltered. But then she remembered her mother's voice—calm, steady, certain.

Susie closed her eyes and let the letter fall into the flames.

The fire caught instantly. The paper curled and blackened, the ink running into oblivion as the words dissolved into smoke.

She knelt there, unmoving, until nothing but ashes remained.

Reaching once more into the trunk, her fingers brushed something small and cold.

Sam's wedding ring.

She lifted it into her palm—the simple gold band

shining faintly in the firelight.

Susie turned it over in her fingers, feeling the weight of everything it represented.

After a long, silent moment, she slipped the ring into her pocket.

She closed the trunk slowly, sealing away what little remained.

The fire crackled quietly behind her, the last evidence of a life carefully erased, just as Eliza had asked.

Susie rose to her feet, her heart breaking but sure.

She had kept her promise.

Without looking back, she crossed the room and gently closed the door behind her.

♦ ♦ ♦ ♦ ♦ ♦

The cemetery was quiet, the winter air was sharp and raw.

Bare branches swayed in the cold wind, and the sun dipped low behind a veil of gray clouds. A much older Ann Boyers and a handful of friends and family members huddled around the open grave, their heads bowed against the chill as the preacher spoke in a low, solemn voice.

"Though we commit her body to the earth," the preacher intoned gently, "her spirit rests in the hands of our Lord."

Elmore stood with his arm around Susie's shoulders, his hand firm and reassuring against her slight frame. Susie stared blankly at the open grave, her heart numb, the world around her fading into a dull, colorless haze.

The preacher offered a final blessing, and the grave

diggers stepped forward, shovels in hand.

The first clump of earth fell onto the coffin with a heavy, hollow thud.

Susie reached slowly into her pocket and pulled out the small gold ring. The metal felt cold against her palm.

Without a word, she stepped forward.

Standing at the very edge of the grave, she held the ring above the open earth. For a long moment, she hesitated.

Then, with a soft, steady breath, she let the ring fall.

It landed with a faint metallic clink on the wooden coffin below, a sound so slight it almost disappeared into the growing wind.

As the grave diggers continued their work, the soil buried the ring from sight, swallowing it whole.

Elmore watched her, but he said nothing. Some things did not need words.

Susie folded her arms tightly across her chest and stepped back, her eyes never leaving the grave as the final shovelfuls of dirt fell into place.

Ann stood nearby, her face pale and etched with quiet sorrow. She wrapped her arms around Elmore in a tight, comforting hug. One by one, the mourners walked away, their quiet murmurs fading into the cold wind. A few whispered words, a few brief nods, and then they were gone.

Susie waited.

She stood before the fresh, unmarked mound of dirt, her breath misting in the sharp air.

Elmore approached quietly, laying a gentle hand on her shoulder.

"Come on, Susie," he said softly. "Let's go home."

Susie nodded, though her gaze remained fixed on the grave.

"Goodbye, Momma," she whispered.

At last, she turned and walked away with her father, the cold wind brushing against her face, tugging at her skirt as they moved across the empty cemetery.

Behind them, the unmarked grave sat in solemn solitude, the earth freshly turned and bare.

High above, a lone raven circled, its black wings cutting starkly against the pale winter sky.

With a sharp caw, it swooped lower, gliding gracefully before perching atop the mound of loosened dirt.

The bird sat there, silent and still, like a sentinel.

The wind quieted, leaving only the faint rustle of leaves as the raven remained, watching, guarding. Though Eliza Allen had wished to slip quietly from memory, history would not let her go.

Epilogue

Eliza Allen's grave remained unmarked for more than a century, just as she had wished.

It wasn't until generations later that the family, seeking to honor her life in their own quiet way, placed a small marker on the site—a simple stone bearing only her name and dates, a gesture of remembrance rather than renown.

As for Sam Houston, his life continued to carve itself into the fabric of American history.

After his triumph at San Jacinto, he served as the first President of the Republic of Texas, then later as a Senator after Texas entered the Union. In his final years, he was elected Governor of Texas, though he would famously oppose the state's secession from the Union—a decision that cost him dearly.

He died in 1863, his body weary but his legacy undeniable.

The city of Houston, Texas—now one of the largest and most vibrant cities in America—stands as a living testament to the complicated, larger-than-life man who once dreamed of even greater things.

Author's Note

The events surrounding Sam Houston and Eliza Allen are shrouded in a great deal of mystery and speculation. What we do know for certain is that their relationship, brief as it was, has left a lasting impact on both their lives and on the history of Tennessee.

In 1829, Sam Houston, then the Governor of Tennessee, began a courtship of Eliza Allen, the daughter of the prominent Allen family in Gallatin. Their engagement was met with much excitement, as the pairing of the ambitious politician and the young, beautiful Eliza seemed a fitting match. However, the details of their relationship are not entirely clear. What we do know is that the two were married in a private ceremony, but only months later, their union was abruptly dissolved.

The reasons for their separation have never been definitively explained, and the truth behind it remains a subject of much speculation. Some historians believe that personal differences, exacerbated by Houston's tumultuous political career and personal struggles, led to the breakdown of their marriage. Others suggest that Eliza's dissatisfaction with the relationship, or perhaps another man played a larger role in the split.

What is certain, however, is that after the divorce, Houston's public persona shifted after fleeing Nashville to live with the Cherokee. His marriage to Eliza, though short-lived, is often considered a pivotal moment in his life. The end of the union seemed to fuel his rise to national prominence, cementing his place as a larger-than-life figure in the history of Texas and the American frontier. Some even say that the pain of the divorce propelled him into his legendary status, as it was shortly thereafter that he moved west and began the campaign that would eventually lead to his leadership in Texas and his role in its fight for independence.

As for Eliza, her life after the divorce is even more mysterious. Little is known of her personal reflections during that time, though it is clear that the event shaped her in profound ways. The historical records regarding her life post-marriage are sparse, and she remains a somewhat elusive figure in the annals of history. Despite her marriage to Houston and eventually Elmore Douglas, Eliza's role in her own right, and the influence she may have had, remains largely overlooked by mainstream narratives.

What we do know, however, is that no one truly knows what happened between Sam and Eliza. The exact nature of their marriage, the reasons for their separation, and how it shaped their futures is something that has been lost to time. Much of their relationship remains open to interpretation, adding a layer of mystery and intrigue to both of their lives. This narrative, much like their story, is an exploration of what might have been, built on the scant details we have and the wide unknowns that continue to capture the imagination.